NIGHT WIND

Russell Williams

InfusedMedia Co. LLC
www.infusedmedia.co
1-888-251-6088

CHAPTER ONE

As the story opens, T.P. is driving down a lonely country road enroute to the mansion of his foster parent, whom is giving T.P. a birthday party for his 26th birthday. The road is long and narrow with overlapping trees, which shade the road from the sun. The woods are thick on both sides of the road and accented only with briars. The sounds of creepy crawly wildlife are most prevalent and the rustling of small trees in the midst denotes caution of larger animals constantly on the move. There are many dead trees with fallen branches that still tower and entangle the trees that live and give bloom. The scenery is very gloomy and undesirable except for a person of the dark side. T.P. finds the ride pleasing and anticipates his arrival at the mansion. His reputation triggers a devious plot in his genius but deranged mind. He knows at the mansion, there lies an abundance of wealth and a tremendous supply of power. Until now, he could only get its table scrapes.

T.P. has finally arrived at the gateway to the mansion which is heavily guarded by privately screened armed guards and hi-tech state of the art video equipment. The surveillance camera visually patrols the perimeter of the mansion 24 hours a day seven days a week. The visuals are monitored at the guard house and also inside the mansion. T.P. is greeted at the gate by the guards, at which there is an immediate parking area. He leaves his car and passes through a walk gate which has a metal detector sensor attached. No one drives up to the mansion. Everyone must pass through the sensory gate and be transported to the mansion. There are no exceptions to this rule. As T.P. enters the transport car, the scenery is spectacular and breathe taking. Never would anyone expect to see such beauty in the midst of such gloomy wilderness. The lawn was professionally landscaped with rose gardens and rare vineyards in the midst. There were beautiful man ponds where ducks and rare birds played and chirped in harmony.

While riding in the transport car enroute to the mansion, the driver tries to make small talk with T.P. in the form of birthday greeting and how's your health type pleasantries.

T.P. replies, "Things are going to be all that I want and when I want. The day will come when I shall be master of the game."

Upon his arrival at the mansion, T.P. is greeted by the butler and his coat is received. As T.P. walks into the main ball room of the mansion, there is an extra coldness and tension that fills the room. His foster parent, whose name is Jeff Wielder, greets him with a happy birthday wish and a warm caring hug. Jeff Wielder tell T.P. that this will be a night that he will never forget, for tonight, he assures T.P. that he will get all that is coming to him. Jeff Wielder places his arm around T.P's shoulder and says boastfully, "I have the power to make dreams come true and this I shall do for you." Jeff Wielder and T.P. now entered the section of the ballroom where he is received by the remaining five guests. As T.P. walks slowly into the room to engage the remaining guests, he carries with him a draft that generates shivers throughout as they spontaneously bursted out "Happy Birthday!" This night is for you, "Long live the king." It was as if a window was open and the night wind softly blew through the room. Jeff Wielder ordered his butler to be sure and close the French doors to the courtyard. The night wind was all so very noticeable.

The festivities of the birthday party carried on until 1 am in the morning, even though there was laughter, fun and social drinking in the air, tension in the room reign supreme. All of the guest would seemingly console T.P. about how misfortunes had fallen his way. Also, they told how he was basically misunderstood. But all of this would change as of tonight. They assured him that the best is yet to come.

It was at this time when Jeff Wielder made his announcement to T.P. and all of his guest. Jeff Wielder's announcement went as follows: "Tonight T.P., I will make you a serious part of my life. I will make you my right hand man. I'll make you my prince. After tonight, you will have no worries or problems. No more never T.P. I will solve everything and remove all of your obstacles forever and ever more."

T.P. smiled so innocently and looked so grateful for all that had been said, but in his mind, his silent thoughts ran deep. He knew that no matter what kind of business deals that were to be offered him, he would win it all and they would lose everything. T.P. knew that he peddled invisible coffins that he disguised as super business transactions whereby rewards seem too

great for anyone to turn down. All a person had to do was agree on one and T.P. would bury that person dead or alive. T.P. stopped smiling and said softly, "All of you are too kind and I can't express how much your words mean to me this night. I thank you one and all."

Jeff Wielder then motioned for everyone to come outside where he would give T.P. a birthday gift that would be deserving of his newly made prince. As the guests exited the mansion and stood on the professionally landscaped lawn, a small shiver swept through the crowd as the night wind softly howled as if to say "Happy Birthday T.P." It was at this time when Jeff wielder raised his hands high above his head and snapped his fingers to signal one of his servants who sat farther down the road to the mansion in a parked car. Headlights came on with high and low beams gleaming. To see beyond the headlights was definitely impossible. The car began to come forward until it was in the midst of the crowd of guests. It was a 2003 powder blue Rolls Royce, fully equipped with telephone, wet bar and the works. The driver began to exit the Rolls Royce leaving the engine running. Jeff Wielder then turned to T.P. and said with eyes sparkling, "T.P. this is for you with all of my blessings."

T.P. Smiled as he walked 360 degrees around this new toy, then he turned to Jeff Wielder and told him that, "This truly will be a night that I will never forget." But in TP's mind he knew that this is just only the beginning.

Jeff Wielder replied, "T.P., take it down the road for a test drive and get the feel of your new Rolls and the power that it generates. After you return, we will talk about a multi million dollar venture in which you will reach millionaire status."

T.P. agreed and proceeded to drive the Rolls, leaving the mansion and traveling down the dark and lonely road on which he had come. T.P. was truly enjoying the ride, the lonely road and the power serge that he was feeling. It really felt just due. As T.P. traveled down the road, the night wind became more brisk and chilling as the breeze softly howled through the gloomy overlapping trees.

T.P. was about three miles down the road when without warning, the engine shut down and the Rolls Royce came to a dead halt. The only working parts on the car were the headlights and the light on the car phone. Almost momentarily, the car phone began to ring. T.P. knew at this time that the cheat was about to fall upon himself. What T.P. didn't know was the price tag of the cheat. It could be anything, from a lesson to be learned or the price could be life. T.P. never ever paid the price of the cheat before, he was always the one who carried the cheat and made others pay. This time, just maybe, things might be different.

T.P. sat in a suspenseful calm and proceeded to answer the phone. As he put the phone to his ear, pressing it tightly against the side of his face, he heard Jeff Wielders voice say cheerfully, "T.P. I have more birthday surprises in store for you. Your car is electronically controlled and was programmed to stop in that particular spot. If you would be so kind as to look to your left and to your right, you should see a small shed on both sides of the car."

As T.P. cautiously looked to his left and to his right, he observed the two sheds. Without warning, the doors sprang wide open on each of the two sheds. Out of each shed like cannon balls being fired raced a jet black 2001b. Rottweilder towards each side of his new Rolls Royce. Almost simultaneously the k-9s hit the car causing dents and rocking motions. It felt like being in a small boat at sea during a severe storm. The Rottweilders' heads were so big that they covered 80% of the door windows. Their teeth were long and sharp as they scratched and pressed them against the window panes. Their growls were so loud, fierce and terrifying that only a well made Rolls Royce could muffle the vicious nightmarish sound to that of a lower key. The night wind began to blow harder and harder, while the overlapping trees began to rock and sway as the fierce night wind blew and howled through the branches, as if in fury and anger.

Jeff Wielder continued to talk on the phone saying, "T.P. it sounds like you have met the other part of your birthday gift. They are two of the best trained killer dogs in the world and I give them both to you. Last but not least, look inside the glove compartment. You will find a 9mm pistol and one bullet. You may do with it as you please. Also in the glove compartment is a detonator with digital timer that will blow and kill everything within 20 sq. feet if any portion of it is detached. It will also do the same thing in four minutes after the red light on it begins to flash. Now you shall pay in full for all your evil deeds and most of all T.P. you shall suffer before you die. My five guests and I all contributed to your final birthday party, for you have brought death and suffering to all of our lives. Now it's time for you to pay up in full, you evil bastard."

Suddenly, the light on the timer began to flash and four minutes appeared on the timer. Jeff Wielder bids his joyful farewell, "T.P., you have exactly four minutes to kiss your ass goodbye."

T.P. hangs up the phone as the car rocks from side to side from the taunting of the killer dogs trying to get inside. The killer dogs were trained to rip human flesh apart until dead. This was their job and the killer dogs were more than anxious to get the job done. The evil inside the car began to build as the timer starts the final count down. T.P. knows that he has four minutes to free himself from 20sq. feet of the car, or he must wait for his revenge in hell.

Back at the mansion Jeff Wielder explains that after the explosion, he would have his servants clean up and dispose of all debris from the road. Also, they would remove all traces of T.P.'s body and it would be like he never existed. Jeff Wielder sighed to his friends. "Finally this evil being will be laid to rest." Jeff Wielder and his five closely bonded multi millionaire friends began to reminisce about the deaths and suffering that T.P. had inflicted into their lives, as if to give justification to their acts of vengeance upon him tonight. All of the men had justification and even a debt to humanity to take the life of one as evil as T.P. Everyone wanted to tell their personal story about T.P.'s treachery as if to clear their personal conscience.

Jeff Wielder began his story first about how he became foster parent to T.P. Jeff Wielder sat down in his easy chair, after being served another drink by his butler and began to express his inner feelings of T.P.'s reign of evil. With tears slowly trickling from one eye, while the hand that held his drink slightly trembled Jeff Wielder began to speak.

CHAPTER TWO

WITH A FLUSHED LOOK ON his face, Jeff wielder said, "When T.P. was sixteen years of age there was a fierce electrical thunder storm. It took place in the middle of the night. Lightening struck the home of T.P. and his family causing the house to burst into flames. The fire was so quick and fierce that in less than twenty minutes, the entire two story home was burned completely to the ground. T.P. was the only child. Both his mother and father were burned to death and T.P. at the time was not at home. He arrived on the scene about the same time as the police and fire department. As T.P. stood watching the remains of his parents being removed from the burnage, his face showed no feelings of pain and hurt for what had just taken place. It was almost like he was alienated from the incident. The storm began to cease and chilling night wind began to blow an unearthly howling sound. It was at this time that a streak of lightening raced acrossed the sky, giving light to this heart breaking scene. Seconds later lightening struck again and singled T.P. out of the crowd and struck him direct. People that saw said that his skeletal system could be seen with peculiar deformities to the skull. No one could explain exactly what they meant, but everyone that saw agreed that there was something different. What was harder to explain was that he lived. When the ambulance rushed him to the hospital, he had a bluish glow around his entire body and was left in a coma. T.P. was put in the coma ward where my natural son Eric was because of a head injury from a motorcycle accident. My wife and I would visit my son, but something about T.P. made us want to check on him too. Our son died four days later and we were really hurting with grief. But still there was something that compelled us to keep going back to the hospital to see T.P. I couldn't explain it and neither could my wife."

After pausing for a few seconds, Jeff Wielder continued to explain, "T.P. stayed in coma for twenty- seven days and eighteen hours before he rejoined the real world. By this time, my wife and I had grown attached to him for reasons that we never knew butonly felt. We researched his family and found out that he had no next of kin. After countless visits and talks with T.P., my wife and I decided to adopt him. He seemed quiet and very innocent but yet, he concealed a very dark secret that left you with a yearning to know more of and about him. It was like he possessed a powerful atmosphere that he controlled exclusively. So at the age of sixteen we made our home T.P.'s home. We offered T.P. the best that money could provide private schools, martial art classes, new car and a generous allowance. But T.P. had an evil shell around him that began to prevail and progress rapidly. He always wanted more and his intentions grew despicable."

"At the age of seventeen, he was involved in a drowning death. A dispute between T.P. and another boy occurred while swimming and it was a fierce fight in the water, resulting in the boy being drowned. The camp counselors said that the two of them were submerged for about three minutes before they could retrieve them from the bottom of the lake. The boy died and T.P. lived. The cause of death was not certain. The boy's lungs were filled with water, but his neck was also broken. After paying out $15,000.00 the court ruled self defense. At the age of eighteen, T.P. had an I.Q. of a master genius and could have his pick of any He attended a university in university in the world. England. In the year of his graduation his evil could be felt as well as seen. On graduation night, T.P. received his degree in business law and my wife and I wanted to feel so proud, but something evil in the air was too strong. My wife and I celebrated only shortly with T.P. He made it very clear that he must say farewell to all that he knew while in Europe. We didn't see T.P. until an hour before our flight for America was about to leave. Our flight was scheduled to take off at 9:45 a.m. and as we boarded the plane and awaited take off, T.P. gave some informative news. He told us that at 10:00 a.m. our plane would be flying over the university and he wanted us to see how it looked from the air. Also, he wanted to take pictures to remember it and this time in his life."

"T.P. sat back in his seat and closed his eyes with a small smile upon his face. His devious mind began to back track to what he had done the night before. It reflected the evilness in his soul, and anticipation of some kind of gratitude or satisfaction that's only minutes away. Minutes later, T.P. drew our attention to the window of the plane and said its 9:59 a.m. We should be over the university. One minute later, I could not believe what my eyes had perceived. My wife and I saw every building of the university being blown up and crumble to the ground, leaving only back smoke, fire and despair. T.P. continued to take pictures without showing any alarm or surprise. The entire plane of passengers showed shock and dismay. I bursted out along with the other passengers by saying, who could have done such an evil thing. In the background, I could hear some people screaming, this must be the actions of terrorists. I looked at T.P. and no words had to be said. I could feel the evilness in him and some how knew the truth of the matter. The remainder of the trip home was quiet and desolate. T.P. only slept and showed no desire for conversation. After we returned home, the television and the newspaper were filled with news about the horrible incident. Authorities were thinking terrorist, but had no solid proof or leads. There were two to three bombs placed in each building set to go off at exactly 10:00 a.m. Three security guards were brutally killed and six hundred people perished in the explosions. I knew then that T.P. was totally evil, but I didn't really know what I should do about it. Little did I know that time wasn't on my side. At this time T.P. was twenty four years old."

With tears running from both eyes, Jeff Wielder mourned, "T.P. killed my wife Marian. I have video cameras that cover every room in the mansion, No one knew about them but me. They were for my eyes only."

Jeff Wielder began to shake and tremble as he continued, "I have my wife's murder on tape. T.P. entered the mansion around 2:15 p.m. and I was at my corporate office. The butler I had for ten years, greeted T.P. at the door as usual. T.P. entered and without any hesitation launched a vicious blow to my butler's chest, which made him grab his heart and drop dead on the floor. T.P. then carried him on his shoulder to the top of the stairs only to throw him all the way down the stairs. My wife was up stairs and heard the commotion. Marian rushed out of the bedroom only to see the butler lying at the foot of the stairs and to stand face to face with T.P. Without uttering a word T.P. grabbed my wife by her face and pulled her to him. While clutching her face, T.P. kissed my wife and in the next second, he snapped my wife's neck. He killed her!"

Jeff Wielder broke into a painful cry and his friends could see the inner hurt written all over his tear dripping face. His friends reached out their hand to touch and console him as he began to stand and finish his story.

With a trembling voice Jeff Wielder said, "But that wasn't enough. He draped my wife's dead body over the banister and tore her gown half off. Then while she was still draped over the banister half naked, T.P. raped her dead body and after he was through, he rolled my wife's body down the stairs head first. She landed on top of the butler. Then, T.P. walked slowly down the stairs and when he got to the foot of the stairs, he took my wife's dead hand and scratched the face of my butler, being sure to leave blood and skin underneath my wife's finger nails. He walked out of the door and never looked back. The police ruled that my wife and the butler were involved in a situation of passion, involuntary of course. They concluded that, the butler raped my wife and that the two of them struggled and fell to their deaths. I said nothing to the police about my tape because that kind of evil can't be harnesses or locked up. It must be destroyed. Plus, I swore on my wife's grave that I would see T.P. dead or I would take my own life. Because of my wealth and power, I insisted that the investigation be concluded without an autopsy and kept safe from a great deal of bad publicity. Because of T.P.'s thirst for wealth and power, I knew that I also was marked for the death, If I was to die or be killed, then all of my wealth and power would go to T.P. Therefore, I took extra pain to keep myself safe and well protected. This is why I bit the bullet and bide my time. I wanted T.P.'s death to be horrible and memorable."

Nevertheless, time passed and two months later, T.P. entered a full contract karate tournament. It had a purse of $25,000.00 and some kind of title. There were little or no rules for the winning. T.P. crippled each of his opponents except for one. In the last match for the purse and the title, T.P. killed his opponent in the first minute of the match by running his hand into his opponent's body and compressing his liver. He seems to have an unquenchable thirst for blood, pain and above all death. I wanted him dead! Dead! Dead! It's of Jeff another one of his guest by the name of Jermaine Kenwood spoke so consoling.

"Let me finish," Jeff Wielder spoke out, with both hands now shaking and a tear stained face. "It all begins to come together now. If you remember, I told you that T.P. stayed in a coma for twenty seven days and eighteen hours in total hours, what do you think it would add up to? Well, I'll tell you what it adds up to. It comes to 666 hours. It may be just coincidence but I don't think so. T.P. wears the mark of the beast and we did right my friends in destroying this evil one. But still, the best part of it all was that we made him suffer mentally and physically before his death. We put him in a sure death situation with only alternate ways to die and each one was equally as horrible. He could choose to be ripped apart by the killer dogs until dead, or he could use that one bullet and take his own worthless life. If T.P. takes too long to make up his mind, the bomb will do the job for him."

Jeff Wielder began to laugh as if it brought him pain and joy at the same time. Recomposing himself, Jeff Wielder spoke with gut feeling, "The best part like I said was that we put him in multiple sure death situations and made him wait for death to come.

Silence filled the room and like clock work, Jeff Wielder began to once more laugh which triggered a combustion of laughter that spreaded throughout his guests.

CHAPTER THREE

Jermaine Kenwood broke the laughter while trying to stop laughing himself by saying, "Let us have another toast then I must speak my peace. Now, I too must bury the hatchet."

The butler began to refill the glasses with $400.00 bottles of champagne as Jermaine Kenwood prepared himself to tell his personal story of death and destruction inflicted into his life by T.P.

"My first encounter with T.P's reign of evil and viciousness was bestowed on me through my brother Jamie," Jermaine explained. "My brother Jamie had a diamond mine in Africa and it had done quite well for him. Its total worth was about $400,000,000.00 He was happily married and the father of six. I really loved my brother and he was a real go getter. He would do no harm to no man and his only flaw was that he was too trusting," Jermaine Kenwood said with eyes beginning to water." Jamie had been leaving his corporate office in the evening around 5:00 p. m. for years. It was almost like clock work, day in and day out, always the same way. His chauffeur would be waiting in front with the car and would drive him to his estate. But one day all of that changed. It was on a Tuesday evening around 5:00 p.m. when all hell bursted loose. My brother Jamie was coming out of his corporate office headed for his chauffeur and the car when a black van pulled up. Two men got out of the van and began moving in the direction of the chauffeur. The path of the two men intercepted my brother at his car. One of the men was asking for a light for his cigarette. While the chauffeur was reaching for the lighter, he was stabbed in the chest by one of the men and before he could fall to the ground, the other man cut his throat. The chauffeur was dead before his bleeding body fell onto the concrete pavement. The two men quickly grabbed my brother at knife point and tried to force him into the van. This incident was happening so fast and so timely that it barely drew any attention from the crowd of people going about their normal routine. However, one person happened to be in the area and that one person happened to be paying attention. As you already know, that person was T.P. He quickly sprang into action and pulled a pistol from the coat of his $3000.00 suit and discharged only two rounds. The first bullet struck one of the killers in the temple of his head. He fell dead face down on the pavement with the left side of his face completely missing. The second killer clutched my brother to his chest, while holding the knife to my brother's throat; he muttered these words as if in total shock. What the hell are you doing? T.P. did not reply. Instead, T.P. discharged the second round and the bullet entered the second killer through his right eye which blew the back of his head off and left blood and brains all over the pavement. As quick as it happened, it was over, with two killers and a chauffeur lying down in pools of blood and brains, dead to the world. Jamie was in shock and feeling so obligated and beholding to T.P. for saving his life. It was natural and very understanding that the two of them would become the closet of friends. My brother felt that he owed so much to T.P. and T.P. made him pay in full."

That abduction scene was set up by T.P. and those two killers worked for him. T.P. paid them to kill the chauffeur and pretend to abduct my brother. After Jamie saw his chauffeur brutally killed, he could onlythink the same fate for himself.

At this time, T.P. would intervene and some kind of way scare the killers off. They would then flee and all would end well. That was the plan and only plan that the two killers knew, but T.P. doubled crossed them and killed them both. That's why one of them screamed to T.P., what the hell are you doing? T.P. again covered his tracks and no one could connect the dots to him and his reign of evil. T.P. saw three people dead to only become my brother's closet friend. He values no life in his evilness. Nevertheless, his plan worked. T.P. and Jamie became closer than blood. My brother took him to Africa to check on a problem at his mine and do some game hunting."

Jermaine Kenwood began to sit down and take for himself a couple of minutes of silence. He seemed to feel the need to slow his body functions down in order for him to continue on. Jermaine had the full attention of all the men as they patiently waited for him to proceed.

Jermaine broke the silence by saying, "I suppose you wonder how I know all of this to be fact, well let me finish my dear friends. I hired a private investigator to dig up all he could on the two men that T.P. had killed. The word down under was that someone paid them $5000.00 each to do exactly what I said. There were seven people that knew of this deal and knew that they were doubled crossed. All seven of the men would swear on it, but none would do so in a court of law. The fear for their lives and safety was too great. Deep down inside, the seven men knew that the person they called someone was in reality T.P., but no one dared call out his name. The people down under knew more about T.P.'s evil than we did and we knew enough to want to see him dead. So like Jeff, I too bit the bullet and decided to bide my time as well."

"But getting back to my brother and T.P. whom went to Africa, they were to stay in the country for one week. Two days later Jamie faxed his corporate office with a deed giving T.P. half ownership in his diamond mine and based on the contingency that if anything happened to my brother, T.P. would receive another quarter interest which would give him controlling share. Seventy-five percent of the mine would belong to T.P. and twenty five percent to this surviving family. Jamie did not need the diamond mine because his monetary worth could last his family ten life times, but what he was doing was signing his own execution. I really feared for my brother's safety and I was very doubtful that he would return home alive. I was on pins and needles and I tried numerous times to contact Jamie, but I could never catch him in and none of my phone calls were returned. I began to feel that it might already be too late."

However, Jamie and T.P. returned home to America and I was shocked with joy when I received his phone call from the airport. I told Jamie that I had vital information and we must meet. I expressed great concern that T.P. not know about our meeting, but before I could finish telling him Jamie spoke out with animosity in his voice. He told me that he had no secrets from T.P. After Jermaine Kenwood let go of a few whimpers and pulled a handkerchief from his pocket to clear his nose, he continued once more to speak.

"Is T.P. standing there with you Jamie?" Jermaine asked while clutching the phone tightly in his hand and against his face.

Jamie's reply was, "Of course he is," Jermaine mourned softly while dropping his head, "I hung the phone up without saying another word. My brother never made it from the airport. Jamie was found dead in the men's room. He was sitting on a toilet and the paramedics diagnosed his cause of death to be a heart attack. No one could prove different, but I knew some kind of way T.P. caused my brother's heart to stop beating. T.P. killed my brother and he wanted to take control of his mine. I advised my brother's family to file appeals to contest T.P's right to any claims on the mine. At least, this may tie his hands long enough for me to figure out what to do."

"All in all, I am happy for this night. I have lived and yearned for this moment," Jermaine spoke gently with a smile that began to rise on what was once a stormy tear stained face.

Jermaine ordered another round of champagne as he happily told his friends, "Tonight we have done well. T.P.'s birthday and his death shall always be our memorial day."

Everyone began to applaud as if Jermaine's words had touched their souls and made them feel reborn. Jermaine began to sit down as if a tremendous burden had been lifted from his shoulders. At the same moment, another guest began to take the floor and seek the attention of everyone. His name was David Jennings.

CHAPTER FOUR

"I MUST TAKE MY TURN FRIENDS in pissing on this one so evil," David said laughing. I want to make this toast that T.P. rots in hell forever," shouted David.

Everyone agreed with pleasure. David leans against the mantel and began his personal story about T.P's evil and how it affected his life.

"I carry a lot of hurt and anguish just like the rest of you," David said softly. "But even though, we are still lucky. We have lived not only to talk about T.P.s evilness and toast this memorable occasion, but we all have lived to do something about it. Our dealings with T.P. were not direct and for this, we are truly blessed. All that had direct dealings with T.P. have been brutally killed. Thank your lucky stars my friends because tonight, we will place his soul back in hell where it truly belongs.

"Let me cut you off for just a minute David. Jeff Wielder spoke. "I think I know how T.P. killed Jamie at the airport. T.P. killed my butler with a sharp blow to his chest. I saw on my tape how my butler grabbed for is heart before dropping dead on the floor. The medical report said that he died of a massive heart attack. Therefore, T.P. probably killed Jamie the same way and placed him on the toilet," explained Jeff Wielder.

"Yes, I think the killings were identical," Jermaine said with a pleasing voice. "All of the pieces to the puzzle are fitting just right tonight. I am really enjoying this time and this night," Jermaine declared with astonishing pride.

"David, please continue," Jeff Wielder said with the look of anticipation upon his face.

David turned his drink it his mouth and began taking large gulps until his glass was totally empty. He wiped his mouth with the back of his hand and bowed his head in pain. Everyone knew that David suffered hard and his pain ran deep but now it could be seen all over his face as he began to speak and continue his heart breaking story.

"You all know of my son Kelvin and how much he meant to me," voiced David as he leaned back on the mantel with both arms draped over the top. "My hurt comes from my son and all of his dreams that were flushed down the toilet because of T.P.'s treachery. Kelvin was eight years old and one of the most loveable kids you could ever imagine. His curiosities ran high and strong. Kelvin's thirst for knowledge and meaning went far beyond that of a normal child. His sensitiveness had no boundaries. Kelvin hated hurt and pain, no matter what shape or form it came in. Once a spider entered our home and Kelvin stopped me from squishing it to death. He told me that the spider means no harm and that the spider was just lost. Father let me take the spider outside and put him on the grass, Kelvin had asked me. He was one of the best kids a parent could desire."

David began to walk towards the butler for a refill of the expensive champagne. The rest of his friends watched his every move, for they knew that David was slowly becoming lost inside of his hurt and they wanted to be able to console him as quickly as possible and give him strength to continue his story.

"As I was saying," continued David. "My wife and I could not have anymore children and Kelvin was the last of our blood line. It was up to Kelvin to carry on the family's name into the next generation. I was grooming my son for politics and I had high hopes of one day Kelvin being president. Kelvin would have made a remarkable president with all of the good qualities that he possessed."

"My pain began on a rainy day in September when my chauffeur and my son's nanny went to pick Kelvin up from school. It was a private school for gifted children."

David's eyes were red and juicy with tears that he constantly tried to contain. The pain and hurt in his soul was rapidly building and everyone could see and feel his destroyed inner emotions.

"Excuse me my friends if I stop ever so often, but this is very hard for me to talk about," David explained with tears beginning to over flow. "On that rainy day, my son's teacher was bringing my son to his nanny and the chauffeur when the wind began to pick up and blow harder with a howling sound. His teacher said that she could feel the presence of something evil, but she knew not what. As my son was entering the limo with his nanny a man with a long cloak and hood that covered his face forced his way into the limo also. The limo quickly pulled away. The teacher immediately called the police based on gut feeling and what she had partially seen. The police responded and found the limo about six blocks away. The chauffeur and the nanny had been shot to death and there were no traces of my son to be found. My wife and I were terrified with fear, for we knew not the safety and condition of our only child. Kelvin was all that we had and we loved and cherished him more than life itself. About three days had past and still there was no word about our missing son. I knew of T.P. and the type of atmosphere that he generated, but there were no traces of T.P. or any clues to be found. I could not say for certain that he was the villain, but deep in my heart, I felt that my life had just been cursed by T.P.'s evilness. On the fourth day of my son's abduction, I received a phone call that gave nothing but demands and maybe a possible solution. The voice on the phone seem dismal and in the background, I could hear drafty sounds of the wind blowing through cracks. The presence of evil, I could feel being generated through the phone. I never had close association with T.P., but based on what I have heard about him, it was very possible and believable that T.P. was behind it all.

"Nevertheless, the abductor wanted one million dollars ransom and it was to be in denominations of fifties and hundreds. I was told that I had three days to put the cash together and it didn't matter whether the police were informed about it or not. The abductor told me, the more people that I tell the more chances of someone making a costly mistake. He told me that the first time someone fucks up, he would cut my son's throat from ear to ear and leave him hanging by his feet, up side down to bleed to death like a pig in slaughter. I asked him if I could talk to my son to be sure that he is alive and well. The abductor told me that he would call back in three days at the same time and if I have the cash together, I would be given instructions and I could say hello to my son. But if I didn't have the cash together, I could tell my son goodbye and listen to him scream as his throat is being cut. The entire conversation lasted less than a minute and the abductor hung up the phone. My wife and I were terrified. We knew our son was in the hands of someone evil. Our prayers were to let anyone be our son's abductor except T.P. We had heard that T.P. was totally evil and we knew that he wouldn't hesitate to kill our son regardless of the slightest mistake. Even if everything is done according to instruction, T.P. was evil enough to still kill or cripple our son."

David began to grab his stomach as if what he was saying pierced his gut like a sharp dagger.

"Are you alright David?" One of the guest by the name of Thomas Mason shouted out.

"Sit down for a few minutes David. We all know what you are going through," Jeff Wielder said while trying to offer some assistance.

"No, no, I'll be alright. Let me have another drink of champagne and then I can finish my story once and for all," David told his friends.

All of David's friends joined him in another round of cheer and each of them tried to give David offerings of their strength and compassion.

David began to continue once more by saying, "Well, I had no trouble putting the money together. I didn't have to leave the house. I had the money ready for pick up the very first day and I was hopeful that he would call earlier then the three days as promised. Later, I learned that the three days were given to me not for my benefit but for the abductor's benefit. The three days that we waited were horrible. It was tearing me apart and driving my wife insane. My wife would wake several times during the night screaming Kelvin's name and our family doctor was put on twenty four hour call. To say the least, I wasn't much better. I went through two bottles of nerve pills. It was just awful, believe me, just awful."Finally, the waiting period was over and we received a phone call as promised. As the phone rang, a cold chill shot up my spine, for I knew the moment of truth would be decided this very day. I picked up the phone and before I could say hello, the cold feeling less voice said, do you have the money? I was so eager to say yes that I almost became tongue tied. Time he heard me say yes, the abductor told me that I would receive two phone calls. One would be for entertainment purposes and the other one would be strictly business with no margin for error. Then he slammed the phone to the receiver. One minute later, the phone began to ring and when I picked it up, it was my beloved son Kelvin. The sound of his voice brought tears to my eyes a warm soothing to my chilled weaken body. I asked Kelvin if he was ok. He said that he was fine and all of sudden he began to cry and say how scared he was. Without warning, we were disconnected by the abductor which left my body and mind in total rage. I mentally put myself in my son's place and my body began to tremble at the thought of how frighten he must be. An hour had passed before the phone began to ring again. I quickly answered the phone and the abductor told me to listen very closely, for he gave instructions only once. He told me that I was not to leave the house. The abductor wanted me by the phone in case someone fucked up. He wanted me to hear my son's scream as his throat was being cut. The abductor demanded that my wife be the carrier of the ransom money. She was to deliver the money to 49th and Parkway and have a seat on the beach to wait further instructions. If my wife is followed or any portion of her body is wired, the abductor told me that I would receive another phone call and I can listen to my son scream for his life. As long as I didn't receive a phone call, my son would be safe. Also, the abductor told me that my wife would be searched for wires somewhere on her destination course, so I was to be sure and have her wear clean red lace panties. It was 5 p. m. and I was instructed to have my wife there at 6:45 p.m. No earlier and no later. Finally, the abductor told me in a cold and nasty voice, the stakes are high, so play to win. He assured me that the penalty for error was death, so let the games begin. Those words still echo throughout my soul just like it was yesterday,' cried out David.

"David, if you don't want to go on, you don't have to. I can feel your hurt and sorrow," said Jermaine with tears now rolling down his face.

"No, I must finish my story. I must finish the game," explained David as he tried to recompose himself.

David began to speak slow and soft, "My wife arrived at the corner of 49th and Parkway and proceeded to siton the bench. At the bench there was a pay phone and at 6:45 it began to ring. My wife assumed that the phone call was for her and nervously answered the phone. It was the abductor and she was instructed to take a cab down to 129th and Kings Street and go into a massage parlor by the name Mama's Care, then ask for Samantha and follow her instructions. My wife was to be there no later then 7:30p.m., so quickly she began to flag down cabs in her desperate pursuit to do exactly as she was told. My wife Kathy knew that no mistakes would be tolerated and everything had to be done just right and by the numbers. We both knew that this was our one and only chance to get our son back home alive. Finally, Kathy arrived at Mama's Care massage parlor. It was a shady looking building located in the run down section of town. Crime rate and murders were high in that section of the city. Nevertheless, Kathy entered the massage parlor and the door was locked behind her. As far as Kathy could tell, there was only one person in the parlor, and the woman introduced herself as Samantha. Samantha then pulled out a black rag and began to blind fold my wife. Rage and fear was constantly running wild through my wife's body, for she knew not what to expect next."

David dropped to his knees and bursted into a deep painful cry that made all of his friends feel his inner hurt, while being engrossed in a state of helplessness. His friends raced quickly to his side to share his hurt and to offer him comfort in his hour of pain. Jeff and Jermaine aided David back to his feet.

"I'm o.k. and thanks my friends," bursted out David while he tried to steady his voice in order to continue his story.

As I was saying, "The woman blind folded Kathy and guided her into the back room."

Samantha, another voice spoke out, "Undress the bitch and check her for wires, while I check the money for accuracy. The money is just like it should be, so far you have done well Kathy. You have my congratulations and I shall reward you personally for your efforts," the abductor said in a cold low voice.

My wife then heard the abductor's voice once more say, "Samantha, your work here is done and in the next second, the beginning of a loud scream was cut short by a gun shot. The sound of the blast from the gun had been muffled by a silencer and moments later, the fall of Samantha's dead body could be heard hitting the floor. My wife, while still blind folded, was in total shock and feared that her life would be taken next. She wanted to know, what was going to happen to her? The abductor told her to stand still and listen. He ordered Kathy not to remove the blindfold as he began to run his hands up her dress and slide her red lace panties down to her feet. After removing Kathy's panties, the abductor guided her over to cot and laid her down. My wife told me that she could feel his coldness and a draft all over her body which caused her to shiver with chills. Kathy said, all of this she could feel even before the abductor had touched her body. Then he caressed my wife's body all over so gently, but this lasted only for a few seconds until penetration was achieved. Then, the rape began, full of roughness, pain, rapid pounding of her vagina as he stretched and tore my wife's vagina with his enormous size. After he was done with my wife, the abductor left her lying on the cot in severe pain and bleeding from vagina tissue that had been torn, as he transferred the money into something that my wife could hear zip open and shut. The abductor told Kathy to wait ten minutes before taking off the blindfold and getting dressed. He explained to my wife that all of the instructions on what to do next and how to retrieve our son would be in an envelope on the table. He advised Kathy to take caution and follow the instructions carefully. As my wife sat blindfolded, naked, raped, and bleeding, she could hear the abductor leave out of what sounded like a back door entrance. Even though she was sure that he had vacated the premises, the fear of being wrong and the love of our son made her wait for at least twenty five minutes before removing the blindfold. After waiting the twenty five minutes, Kathy snatched the blindfold from her eyes and the very first thing she saw as her eye began to focus was Samantha's dead body on the floor. Samantha's eyes were unclosed and her mouth hung open which overflowed with blood that constantly dripped from the bullet hole in her forehead. Kathy was terrified and quickly dressed her raped battered body. She used the rag that blindfolded her to slow down the bleeding form her vagina. My wife reached for the envelope on the table and carefully read the instructions. The instructions were typed on plain paper and very explicit. It gave the address of a building across town. In bold print it read come alone. After all that Kathy had been through, she still knew not what to expect next, but the moment of truth was at hand and she knew deep in her soul and for the love of our son that she must continue on and finish the game. Kathy didn't waste anytime vacating the massage parlor and frantically started searching for a cab. She had traveled ten blocks or more before securing a cab. The cab driver raced to the address with Kathy pushing him faster and faster all the way. Finally the cab driver and Kathy reached the designated address and Kathy's heart began to pound and beat faster as her eyes unleashed a down pour of suspenseful tears. She instructed the cab driver to wait, but the cabbie insisted that there was always danger lurking in that particular section of town. He advised Kathy that she shouldn't go into that condemned building alone and made her aware of the fact that he could be robbed while he waited for her. Nevertheless, the cabbie told Kathy to pay up front and he would wait as long as he could without putting himself in danger. Kathy agreed and after paying the cabe upfront began to painfully proceed to the condemned building, leaving a drip drop trail of blood that fell from the blindfold rag in her panties, which was overly saturated with blood from her bleeding vagina. The room number was 202 where our son Kelvin was to be found. As my wife entered the building, she stepped high over garbage and internal deterioration. As Kathy slowly climbed the stairs she began to give silent prayers for Kelvin's life and safe return. Finally, she stood face to face with room 202. Kathy began to call out,

Kelvin, Kelvin, but there was no answer. My wife placed her trembling hand on the door knob and with adrenaline soaring high, Kathy slowly turned the knob. As Kathy pushed open the door, all that she sought, her crying eyes now beheld. Kathy fell to her knees and unleashed a scream that could be heard and felt throughout that section of the city. Kathy was the first to see our son Kelvin. He was hanging from the ceiling by his bonded feet, over a pool of blood, naked with his throat cut from ear to ear. After hearing Kathy scream, the cab driver flagged down a passing patrol car and minutes later, the police had the entire building surrounded. When the police entered the building, they found my wife. Kathy was passed out on the floor in a state of shock and terror. My wife now resides in a private mental institution where she can be treated and cared for twenty four hours a day. She lives deep in a state of wonder drugs and the doctors assured me that only an act of God can restore her destroyed mind. There were no facts or clues to link all of this evil to T.P., but deep in my heart I knew that T.P. was behind it all. As I attended my son's funeral, I too took an oath and vowed on Kelvin's grave to see T.P. die a horrible death. A week had passed and the police discovered a man by the name of Henry Moore who laundries money for forty five cents on the dollar, lying dead in his office with his neck and spine broken. Locked up in his vault was one million dollars and it was traced to the money my wife was carrying on her journey into terror. T.P. had exchanged the ransom money and killed Henry Moore in order to guarantee his secrecy. T.P. had won the game, the money and left my life totally destroyed. He left no dots to connect, no traces of evidence and no leads to follow. Nothing did he leave other then death and destruction. Again T.P. was untouchable. So my friends here I stand a lonely broken destroyed man, but tonight I find joy in my pain for we have settled a debt that was long over due. I must sit down now, for all must take their turn and speak their peace. Believe me my friends, voicing your hurt is the only way."

Excluding David, who had just sat down, Jeff Wielder ordered his butler to open more bottles of his private stock champagne as Jeff and the remainder of his friends began to stand. It seemed that an intermission was needed by the men to recompose themselves in order to absorb more hurt and pain from confessions yet to come. The men would alternate going to the bathroom, while trying to promote gestures of laughter to use as bandages for their many open non healing wounds.

CHAPTER FIVE

Tʜᴏᴍᴀs Fʀᴇᴇᴍᴀɴ, ᴡʜᴏᴍ ᴡɪʟʟ ʙᴇ the next person to let his heart bleed in hopes of all his pain being drained from his soul, tried to make a joke.

"Listen up my friends, we must be sure to save a drink for T.P., therefore I suggest we all take turns pissing some of this fine champagne on his burnt remains," said Thomas with a watery smile on his face.

Laughter keyed up unanimously, the meant to be joke was taken seriously by one and all.

"This we will do, for it makes my soul feel better and my hurt lessens just thinking about it, "Jeff Wielder blurted out while jumping for joy. "But nevertheless, lets settle down my friends and prepare to begin again, for now Thomas must walk the burning coals of pain and hurt to tell of his personal grief and destruction that was inflicted by that bastard T.P."

Thomas began to walk to the center of the room as his face began to transform into a visual mirror of his inner pain. His body began to droop and his face began to rapidly perspire as he turned to face his friends. Thomas projected the look of a man that was about to be executed for a hideous crime that he never committed. He was weakening rapidly and all his friends could see.

David held out his hand to Thomas and said, "I know it's hard to say what you really feel, but in order to get over it, you must first let your pain outward. You must let go. It's the only way. Thomas we are all with you and I know you can do it. You must finish the game."

"Yes David, I must and I will finish the game," Thomas spoke with a trembling voice, while letting go of David's hand. Thomas continued by saying, "Before my father died one year ago, he was an articulate art collector. The most priceless piece of art to have ever been in his art collection was the famed Mona Lisa. He was only to possess its beauty and legacy for a period of one month. For this honor and privilege, my father paid 1.5 million dollars. To behold such a work of art was my father's life time dream come true. My father's estate had maximum state of the art security. Only close members of the family could gain entry. No business or friendly socials were conducted at the mansion. Other then my wife, my daughter and myself, no visitors had been allowed to his estate in the last seven years. My father used his strict security for the purpose of enjoying life as he chose. One that was free of pain and the problems of the world. My father and mother had forty five years of closely bonded marriage which left no need for the outside world. My father's and mother's deep underlying love for each other and my father's art completely fulfilled the two of their lives and their world. Their bond was so closely knitted that one could not live without the other. It was as if the two of them shared only one life to be divided between their two lovingly aging bodies. My parents had done well by all mankind. They had seven shelters where the homeless could come to in their time of need. I'm talking free shelters, clothing and hot meals three times a day, all for just asking. No one needing help was turned down or refused. There were countless youth programs that my parents would sponsor totally, and the only gratitude they sought in return was making a difference where there was none."

"Four days after my father received his cherished work of art, he had a massive heart attack while he and my mother sat quietly viewing the famed Mona Lisa. My father died almost instantly and for the first time in my mother's life, she was all alone. The tragedy was so severe that we had to have two separate funerals for my father. One especially for my mother in which we could only use my father's picture, for my mother could not endure the reality of having my father's body in her presence and seeing him that way. The second funeral was the real one, which included the burial. My mother was really grief stricken and I knew that shortly my mother would soon be joining my father in the grave. There was nothing I could do or say that would make any type of difference. I felt so helpless and all of the money and power that I possessed was worthless in being a deterrent to this devastating occurrence in my life. Both of my parents, whom I've loved and admired all of my life were soon to be lost to the grave back to back. For myself, I could find no rest or peace of mind. I desperately needed to find a quick solution that would restore my mother's will to live."

"However, one week later a package for my mother was delivered to the mansion. It contained a note which instructed my mother to play the cassette at once. The note and the cassette were from a psychic named Hanna, who claimed that my deceased father was trying to make a spiritual connection with my mother through her mediator. On the cassette was my father's voice saying to my mother, Irene you must be strong, you must carry on at all cost. The tape was very clear for the exception of the part where my father's voice had spoken. That portion of the tape sounded identical to my father's voice, but it seemed to have been in a distant windy atmosphere. Also, the tape supplied information regarding the psychic's address and phone number It also implied that my deceased father had much more to relay to my mother and he insisted that my mother should tell no one, for he would not make the trip across again. My father's wishes prescribed that this be scared and not exploited or made a mockery of by others. No one was to know until the time was right. My mother agreed obviously because I was the last to know."

"Immediately after hearing my father's voice, my mother began to bloom and draw strength from the tape that she couldn't obtain from any other source. She made the phone call and reached out to touch the dark side for her salvation. My mother Irene was going to live and go forward with her life as never before. She now had purpose which brought back all of the wonderful treasures of life that were loss with the passing of my father. At this point, I had no knowledge of what or how this drastic change had come to be. All I knew was that it was miraculous and my prayers had been answered. As my mother Irene made the phone call to Hanna the psychic, little did she know that Hanna and her mediator were waiting with great anticipation. The phone call between Hanna and mother proved to be most rewarding and gratifying to my mother. Hanna explained to my mother that my father wanted her to stay strong and live happy." He wanted her to know that even through death; he would remain with her and by her side. Hanna told how may father's feelings were so strong and ran so deep that it enabled him to have the power to communicate and be active among the living, but it must be done a certain way. It must be done in total secrecy. It was for my mother's needs and pleasures only that my father chose to fulfill. To let others know about this would only disrupt my mother's life of tranquility causing exploitation and confusion. Hanna went on to elaborate about the countless phonies and tricks of the trade that are often found in her gifted profession.

Hanna said, "These false prophets give honest gifted psychics a bad name and bring dishonor to those that are truly blessed with this art. In the shops of the false prophets are all sorts of gimmicks and equipment that would be used to create Illusions for monetary gain only. This is certainly not the case with me and whenever time permits. I expose them to the public. Irene, you may feel free to come to my shop for your spiritual connection with your late husband or it can be done in the total privacy of your home. If you choose for it to take place in your home, I need only bring my mediator, no gimmicks, tricks, or equipment. I feel that your late husband would prefer it that way. However, you may come to my shop if it pleases you but I can't control the amount of attention that your coming here would attract. After all Irene, you and your family are very important figures in the social world. Hanna stated her fees are due in full. If for any reason at the end of any session total satisfaction and believability has not been achieved, then Irene you will owe nothing. Instead you will be paid one thousand dollars and all sessions will end," Hanna stated. "Hanna informed my mother that she must decide this matter and let her know the results of her decision within two days, for after that period all may be lost forever. My mother, after experiencing the dramatic change and rebirth of life deep in her soul, eagerly gave a yes answer to Hanna and arranged for a session to take place that very night. Hanna and her mediator were to be picked up at seven p.m. by my mother's chauffeur. For the first time in seven years, visitors were to be accepted at the mansion," Thomas said in a low broken hearted tone of voice.

Irene began to make physical and mental preparations for an evening that bares promise of being reunited with all that was once thought to be lost forever. She really believed in Hanna and looked forward to some form of resurrection of her deceased beloved husband. By 6 p.m. Irene's preparations were complete. She wore a $12,000.00 garment which was always favored by her late husband, diamond necklace with earrings and a matching bracelet. Her hair was made beautifully ready by her on staff beautician and the look of radiance glowed from her face as she descended down the spiral stair case enroute to the parlor. Irene sat in a chair that possessed the look and quality deserving of a queen. She then instructed her chauffeur on his quest and demanded that he return quickly and safely with her long awaited visitors. Irene ordered her butler to prepare and serve tea made with the finest blends of the orient as she awaited the arrival of her guest.

As the clock ticks only a minute from 7 p.m., the long white limo pulls up in front of Hanna's place. Without delay, Hanna and her mediator exited the shop and entered the limo. Hanna was dressed in a long white garment with strings of black beads around her neck. She wore black leather boots that were just below her knees and long black gloves that partially covered a tattoo of a snake on her right forearm. Hanna's mediator was a male and he dressed in a full length black robe with a matching hood that he kept draped over his bowed head which hid 90% of his face. The ride back to the mansion was non conversational. Not a single word was spoken. The chauffeur that transported them to and from the mansion remembers a peculiar drafty atmosphere that could only be felt in the presence of those two passengers. The limo streaked through the city streets and under neon lights destined for the mansion in the suburbs. Irene sat patiently waiting while trying to match a face to the voice of Hanna. She was full of joy and anticipation of what was yet to be. Irene was like a young child on Christmas Eve, constantly sending her butler to the door to check on cars that she only imagined had driven to her door. Finally, that long awaited moment had come to be. The limo pulled to the gate entrance that leads to the mansion. It only stopped momentarily and two arm guards at the gate seated themselves beside the chauffeur as the limo continued on to the mansion. As the limo slowly pulled in front of the mansion, the entrance door was being opened by the butler. The arm guards were the first to exit the car. After opening the doors for Hanna and her mediator, the guards instructed them to not take offense, for both must searched for weaponry and deceit prior to entering the mansion. Hanna assured the guards that no offense would be taken. Her mediator never spoke but constantly kept his head bowed and draped. As the limo slowly pulled away, Hanna, the mediator and the two guards entered the mansion and were received by the butler who stood waiting. The guards took seats in the immediate room, while the butler announced the presence of the visitors and lead them into the parlor. Irene now stood face to face with her visitors and before any pleasantries could be exchanged, the drafted atmosphere seem to overwhelm Irene. Shivers embraced Irene's body as she mentally acknowledged the presence of something strong and some what frightening. She knew at this point, that these were not ordinary people. If what was to take place here tonight could be done, Irene felt confident that the power was possessed by one of her visitors. Irene began to come closer to her mysterious visitors and with her hand extended. She began her introduction. Hanna reached for Irene's extended hand and while holding it gently, she assured Irene that it would be a successful night and she was very honored for being able to serve her. Hanna then introduced her mediator to Irene and told her that for the connection with the after life, the mediator can not have a name. He would simply be referred to as the mediator.

The mediator then stepped closer, with his head still bowed and the hood of his black robe covering 90% of his face, enclosed Irene's hand in his. Irene immediately felt the drastic difference in their touch and cold chills began to race back and forth through out her body. Irene could feel the powerful atmosphere of the mediator which seems to create the presence of drafted air circulating in the room. Hanna could see the transformation taking place in Irene and could very easily identify with it. She too found the atmosphere of the mediator powerful and some what unearthly, but for the money, Hanna was willing to suffer the exposure. Hanna tried to break Irene away from her state of helplessness by asking Irene if something was wrong. Irene immediately expressed how much power was generated by the mediator and demanded to see his face at once. The mediator informed Irene not to be afraid, for he is pure in heart but gifted with powers of the super natural. The mediator then removed his hood and looked Irene directly in her eyes. Irene gave the look of breathlessness. She saw the face of a man that was so handsome, he could be called beautiful His face was so innocent, warm and pure, that Irene could not help but believe in him as he told her to trust and feel safe in his obvious atmosphere. Irene, after being enchanted by the face and consoling words of the mediator, began to ask questions. She wanted to know how does the connection with her late husband work and how soon can it begin? Hanna explained, "We must always begin at the beginning. First, we try to connect from this very room, but if the communication is not strong enough, we must adjourn to another room that was dear to your late beloved husband. Also, in that special room, we will need something material that your late husband valued or cherished most of all. But first, let us try right here and right now. All you have to do is sit in your favorite chair, open up your heart and let your true feelings flow." Irene, Hanna spoke softly, "You may hear the sound of the wind and the howling of the wind, but you need not be afraid. You are very safe and your husband loves you dearly."

"Everyone must be seated for it is time to begin," instructed Hanna. Irene sat in her favorite chair and Hanna sat beside her while holding Irene's hand. The mediator sat on the floor facing the two of them with his legs crossed and tightly pulled to his body. He then pulled his hood over his bowed head and told Hanna to begin.

Thomas began to break down and lose his inner self esteem, for the story he was trying to tell was of his beloved mother.

"I can't go on with my story of destruction, the hurt and pain is too deep", cried out Thomas. "T.P. made my mother experience the horrors and terrors of hell. It's for his death only that I found strength to go on living," mourned Thomas as he covered his face with his hands while dropping slowly to the floor. Jeff Wielder began to move toward Thomas in hopes of being some sort of comfort, when he was grabbed by the arm and stopped by David.

"No, this is not the way Jeff," shouted David. "Thomas, you must face this hurt head on. I felt the same hurt for my son Kelvin, but voicing my hurt here tonight gave me an inner peace that can only come by bleeding your soul," explained David. "You can't stop Thomas, you must continue to bleed and let all of your pain diminish. This is the only way and you may never get this chance again. Trust me Thomas, for yourself and for your beloved mother, you must go on. Thomas, you must finish the game, "David said softly as he extended his hand to Thomas.

Thomas began to rise to his feet while clutching the hand of David.

"I know your words have truth and I do believe that pouring out my heart is the only way," Thomas spoke in a sniffing voice. "Bare with me my friends, for I never was a strong man and now I feel barely a man at all. I will try once more to finish the game," smirked Thomas as he wiped the tears from his eyes with the side of his fingers.

"T.P. is the rot in your gut from which your cancerous hurt and pain grows rapidly," intruded David. "Don't call that evil bastard a mediator. Call out his name and heal yourself Thomas. Rejoice in the sound of his name, for tonight, T.P.'s evil soul will roast in hell," David said so consoling.

All of the men began once more to put their hands together in applause. Even though Thomas had the floor, David had everyone's vote of confidence.

"I will try once more to finish the game my friends," said Thomas. Also I will call out T.P. by name instead of using the word mediator. As I was saying, continuing Thomas, T.P. told Hanna to begin."

While Hanna was holding Irene's hand, she instructed Irene to chant her late husband's name. Irene began to chant Jonathan, Jonathan, Jonathan and at the same time, Hanna began chanting in a language that she made up and devised for this particular occasion which really had no significant.

After about two minutes of chanting, the atmosphere in the room began to change. The presence of a chilling breeze was beginning to circulate within the room. The crystal chandelier began to sway and tingle as the doors to the parlor began to shake and tremble. The night wind became more brisk and chilling as T.P. raised his hands towards the ceiling and began to sling his head from side to side which made the night wind begin to howl as it swirled around the room. Pictures on the wall began to clatter and large mirrors trimmed in gold began to fog.

Irene began to clutch tighter the hand of Hanna while her breathing deepened. The expectation of connecting with her late husband was the only defense Irene had to surpass the fright that was building and growing throughout her body.

Hanna the psychic by no means was any better off as she squeezed tighter the hand of Irene. Never before had Hanna seen and felt so much force projected by one person without the aid of trickery. She knew that T.P. was in touch with super natural powers. The night wind had set the stage for T.P.'s performance.

T.P. suddenly stopped swaying his head from side to side as if something or someone had just entered his body and taken control. The night wind began to lessen and its howl began to soften as T.P. called out, "Irene I love you," in the identical voice of her late husband.

"T.P.'s evil gifts were profound. As a child growing up, he could imitate anybody's voice with perfection. If at all possible, animal sounds he could do even better," Thomas began to explain.

"Yes, you are so right Thomas," Jeff Wielder confirmed. "At the age of sixteen his favorite was a leopard He used to keep my wife and staff petrified with life like imitation.

"As you can see Thomas, the more each of us talk and share our grief, the stronger and the more knowledgeable we all became in piecing together the total picture of T.P.'s evilness, Jermaine spoke with sincerity.

"It's true the more I talk about my hurt the more I feel relieved of its pain." Thomas spoke out. "Let us refill our glasses with more champagne and then once more I shall continue on with my story," Thomas said while extending his crystal glass towards the butler.

Thomas took a large sip of champagne from his glass and began to once more finish his story of horror.

T.P. began to speak out again in the voice of Irene's late husband, calling Irene, Irene, I can't hold on, I'm slipping back into....... As the voice of Jonathan began to softly fade the night wind bursted into a rage of forcefulness. Pictures and ornaments were blown off the wall while curtains waved like flags in the midst of a chilling north wind. Hanna and Irene both grabbed and held each other tightly.

Irene felt safe in Hanna's embrace because she assumed that Hanna had been through this before and knew what to expect. Hanna felt safe in Irene's embraced because she was frightened and knew not what to expect.

Suddenly, the night wind seized and left a cold drafty atmosphere in the room. The curtains that were blown loose began to pile on the floor as they dropped from the windows and there were ornaments scattered around the floor, some of which were broken and totally destroyed. As Irene and Hanna disengaged their embrace and slowly looked around the room, the two of them truly believed that Jonathan had made his presence known and most of all it was done without the aide of trickery. Hanna and Irene turned to face T.P. and there was no doubt in either of their minds that T.P. was real and truly the possessor super natural powers. After seeing how overwhelmed Hanna was, T.P. quickly took charge.

Irene, T. P. spoke so gently "Please don't be alarmed by what you have just witnessed." Your husband was fading back to the other side and in his desperate attempt to stay with us he was exerting all of the forces and power that he could muster.

T.P. continued to talk a he looked Irene directly in the eyes with a serious penetrating effect. He definitely had Irene's undivided attention. T.P. informed Irene that even though her late husband lost the power to speak, Jonathan was about to disclose a secrete wish that he wanted her to fulfill. T.P. instructed Irene that once this special desire of her husband is complete, she would no longer need the services of their special gift.

After recomposing herself, Hanna began to join in the conversation. She assured Irene that she would be able to communicate with Jonathan without any outside help and it would be most pleasant.

Irene began to voice her inner feelings of that mystical moment. "No matter what I have to do to be reunited with Jonathan and fulfill his wishes, you need only tell me "Irene said with pride and commitment.

T.P. said, "In order to advance to the next and final level Irene, I need to know your husband's most dearest room and his most valued possession." In order to totally reunite Jonathan with you forever Irene, our next and final session must be conducted in that special room with Jonathan's most valued possession. There is simply no other way that the unification can be achieved," explained T.P.

Irene sat back in her favorite chair in a peaceful calm and smiled as if in a world of ecstasy." The room most dearest to my husband was the art room and his most cherished possession was the famed Mona Lisa," Irene said softly. "We were in the art room viewing the Mona Lisa when my beloved Jonathan briefly left my life," continued Irene.

T.P. assured that only one more session would be needed to complete the union and it must be done in the art room near the Mona Lisa. T.P. walked closer to Irene and removed his hood while speaking with complete authority.

"We have done enough for tonight, for tomorrow, all that you desire will be fulfilled and our sessions will conclude," T.P. said so gently. "With all of the powers and knowledge that I possess, I promise you that I will reunite you and Jonathan forever and always, then my work will be done," T.P. said so assuringly.

Irene told her visitors how much she believed and trusted them. As they began to leave the parlor, T.P. recovered his head and 90% of his face with the hood of his black robe. As the three of them left the parlor and entered the room where the guards patiently waited, T.P. bursted out in a low key voice, "You may search us now." Irene told the guards that there would be no need for that and further more when the chauffeur picks up T.P. and Hanna; he will be instructed to not stop at the guard house for future searches. The chauffeur was ordered to bring Irene's guest straight to the mansion.

Hanna said, "Both of us thank you for allowing us to serve you in your time of need and if Irene you are truly satisfied then our time here is well spent.

"Yes, I am quite satisfied and for the sake of privacy, I'll pay your fee of one thousand dollars in cash, Irene said eagerly while passing Hanna the envelope which contained the money.

Irene bids her visitors good night and reaffirmed their next and final session, which was to take place the following night. The chauffeur, Hanna and T.P. entered the limo and drove off into the night. The two guards remained stationed inside the mansion, which was their section of security. T.P. and Hanna were dropped off at Hanna's place and during the ride back to the city from the suburbs, not a word was spoken. The chauffeur felt uncomfortable and pressed by T.P.'s unexplainable atmosphere. As the limo slowly pulled in front of Hanna's place, the light on the dimly lit building began to flicker as the night wind swept and hustled trash and debris away from the sidewalk adjacent to the rear door. T.P. and Hanna exited the limo and the chauffeur drove off into the night.

T.P. with his head still bowed and cloaked, turned away from Hanna. As he walked away, there was only silence and the look of two strangers passing in the night.

As the sun began to rise giving birth to a new day, Irene awakened with high hopes and great expectation. She felt deep in her heart that Jonathan would be back in her life. From her bed and between her especially made silk sheets, Irene began to chant Jonathan, Jonathan. But there was only her voice in the midst of silence. No movements no replies. She knew that all of this world would change as of tonight, for she had been assured by a man of great power. After tonight, Irene was 100% sure, that when she called out to Jonathan, he would indeed reply. She knew that all that was lost shall be regained to night and forever.

It was going to be a long and tiring day for Irene because it was the night that could only soothe the itch in her soul.

The clock ticked and time passed slowly. Finally, the time of Irene's salvation was at hand. She sent forth her chauffeur to bring her two visitors without any stops or delays. Irene instructed that there would be no search of her visitors and she wanted them brought directly to her in the art room Irene adjourned to the art room and began her final wait.

The limo began to streak for the inner city destined to retrieve and fulfill Irene's command.

Finally, the limo had returned to the mansion and the butler escorted them straight to the art room, where Irene sat waiting. After all pleasantries hadbeen exchanged and shared,

T.P. reassures Irene that total unification would be completed this night.

Hanna asked Irene if she was ready to begin the final connection with her late husband. Irene expressed the fact that she had been waiting all day and with enormous anticipation. T.P. suggested that Hanna's and Irene's chairs be placed side by side with the backs toward the famed Mona Lisa. He would assume his normal position on the floor facing them and the painting, which should enhance the projections and focus of the connecting powers. Irene and Hanna became seated and T.P. took the position.

Hanna said, "Now we must begin and Irene, you must start chanting your late husband's name. Irene began to chant Jonathan, Jonathan, while Hanna began to chant one her originals devised for the occasion.

T.P. raised his hands high towards the ceiling, while keeping his head bowed and draped. The atmosphere began to transform. As the breeze began to build and circulate around the room, Hanna and Irene began to clutch hands tighter. T.P. began swaying his head from side to side and the night wind began to induce chills while softly howling as if distant. T.P. suddenly stopped swaying his head and gave the appearance of being possessed by some spirit.

T.P. began to speak out as he raised his bowed head. Irene, I have returned to you. I'll never let you be alone to drown in sorrow and grief. For I love you far too much. I have so many vital things to tell you, that I should have told you before and many times over. Time is so precious and yet it is so often taken for granted. I have found a way to make up for the precious time that once was lost. Please Irene, you must tell me with all sincerity whether or not you want me to return to your life. I love you so deeply and I will honor your will. Irene please tell me. I must know.

Irene bursted out with a face full of racing tear drops. I love you Jonathan and I have no life without you. I want us to be together always Jonathan, whether it be life or death, for you are the source of my life. Yes Jonathan, Yes. You must return to my life Jonathan. T.P. began to rise to his feet and walked toward Irene with both hands extended, as he continued to speak in Jonathan's voice. "Irene, come to me and embrace this body that stands before you, for it shall be me, your beloved husband, and we shall be united forever love.

Irene let go of Hanna's hand and began to come forward to meet and embrace T.P. As Irene and T.P. embraced with faces that were pressed cheek to cheek Irene's tears of joy began to slowly run down the side of T.P.'s neck. Chill bumps spreaded from her feet to the top of Irene's head as she clutched T.P. tighter and tighter saying, I love you Jonathan with all my heart and soul. The night wind began to blow harder as it brought its distant howl closer and closer. T.P. began to pull a sterling silver dagger from the sleeve of his robe and he plunged it through the back of Irene's neck until four inches protruded through her throat, he uttered these words. "It is for this moment only that you live. The night wind began to howl like a distant trumpet that was announcing Irene's arrival to the dark side.

T.P. snatched the dagger from Irene's neck and let her limp body fall to the floor as he turned to face Hanna.

The pictures on the wall began to clutter and the door began to tremble against the door jam. Hanna jumped to her feet engrossed in total terror, she began to beg. From ten feet away, T.P. threw the dagger with lightening speed. Hanna dropped to the floor and even though her eyes were wide open, she never saw the dagger coming, which now sets embedded in her face where her nose used to be.

T.P. quickly removed the famed Mona Lisa painting from the frame and rolled it up and placed it beneath his robe. He returned to Irene with a razor that he pulled from his pocket. T.P. kneeled over her body. He cut completely around the border of Irene's face and pealed it off like wall paper. On the canvass where the Mona Lisa once hung, T.P. pasted the face of Irene and in the bottom right corner with the blood of Hanna he wrote Night Wind.

T.P. called out to the butler in Irene's voice and ordered him to have the chauffeur bring the car at once. One of the visitors has to be transported back to the shop to return a package. T.P. continued to talk in Irene's voice saying "I don't want to be disturbed at all until my visitor has returned." Is that clear?" the voice of Irene spoke. "That is perfectly clear" the butler replied. T.P. adjourned downstairs with his hood draped over his face and his head bowed. The butler escorted him to the limo. As the limo raced for the inner city, the visitor was not heard from again. The chauffeur did not return and all of the horror was discovered. The investigation had no leads and the chauffeur was found in front of Hanna's place with his neck and spine broken. The Mona Lisa, as of yet has not be recovered.

"This friends," Thomas blurted out, is my hurt and pain. T.P. destroyed me and my family and there is no legal way to touch him." I never knew hate until I began to hate T. P., Thomas said he bursted out into a loud cry. "You have done well Thomas, David said as all the men came to touch and console Thomas. "Yes, now you shall heal Thomas," Jermaine cried out.

It took a lot of courage to continue your story Thomas, the hurt was tremendous", spoke the fourth guest by the name of Lester Mason. "I only hope that I can show as much courage and stamina as you have shown."

"Don't worry you will do just fine, "Jeff Wielder explained. We all are here to support and aide each other. Tonight, we formed a bond based on death and destruction we've suffered. There is no stronger bond. The experiences we have endured are too great to be handled or housed individually. We must be able to confide in each other and draw strength from our bond as we need it. "Jeff continued.

All of the men began to give applause for they knew Jeff had spoken with truth. They knew that a man so evil as T.P. had to be destroyed for humanity's sake and not only for the suffering and death that he had inflicted into their lives. In order for T.P. to live and survive many people would have to suffer and die a horrible death. They felt more then justified in their actions and there was no remorse what so ever. Jeff Wielder and his friends were in total agreement that if T.P. was to live, then mankind was doomed.

Lester began to ask questions that their were no answers to. How could a person do the things that T.P. has done and yet be a genius? How did he come to be this way? Jeff Wielder, be foster parent tried to make a good stab at the answers.

Jeff Wielder explained, "T.P. is capable of these unearthly things because he is totally evil. simple as that. As far as him coming to be like that the answer is also simple. T.P. was conceived and born in hell. There are no other answers," Jeff said with bitterness. "Jeff, I would like to know something also," Thomas asked. What were T.P.'s real parents like? The ones that were burned to death in the fire. The couple that burned were decent hard working God fearing people. As far as wealth's concerned, they were on the bottom of the totem pole," Jeff explained as he continued to talk. The couple that burned to death were not T.P.'s real parents. After experiencing his evil treachery, I did further research into T.P.'s past. I found that the couple that burned were his foster parents like myself. There was no record of T.P. having real parents. He was found at birth in a garbage can by city trash collectors."

That's where he should have stayed and died David shouted out. "You are so right," Jeff commented but let me finish. "T.P. had a total of six foster parents and all were poor people that couldn't have children by natural birth. They all chose him because of his innocent handsome look. Mysteriously five innocent couples died in fires and in each case the fires were started by lightening. I was the sixth foster parent for T.P. and the only one that was rich and whom didn't burn to death in a fire. Again my friends I say, T.P. wears the mark of the beast and was born in hell.

Lester began to speak, "It does seem quite clear that this is the case, with all that you have said Jeff, T.P. must have been hell sent. Lester continues to talk, "My friends let us have another toast. Let us toast T.P.'s homecoming back to hell.

Everyone began to laugh as they bumped their crystal champagne glasses together.

CHAPTER SIX

"NOW MY FRIENDS, I MUST tell my confession and rid my soul of T.P.'s destruction," Lester Mason said with an uneasiness.

I was once one of the most powerful and richest men in the world and my family name carried clout for generations. As you know, my family for the last 60 years has been in the wrestling profession. We have trained the best of the best. The name Mason means world champion and for the last sixty years a Mason has held the world championship. My family has made billions of dollars through our training camps and by being title holders. T.P. brought all of this to a halt. When T.P. preyed upon my family, not only did he leave death and destruction, he dishonored the family. T.P. made the name Mason a word of total shame that can never be restored. Never!

Lester began to cry and became short of breathe as he spoke these touching words. "I am a man who has no honor and whose family has been put to death and shame forever.

"I had two beautiful children that I loved and cherished. I raised them to be the best anyone could be. They were the best of the best in their chosen profession. They were always taught to be proud of the Mason name and to make it mean more with each passing generation like their ancestors did before them. My kids exceeded my greatest expectations and I loved them dearly," Lester was saying as the lips on his face began to tremble. "Lester take it easy, your hurt runs deep. If you can't continue, we all understand." Jeff spoke out.

Everyone spoke in agreement, for they knew Lester's pain. Everyone in the world knew thanks to T.P.

"No, I must do this," Lester mourned. "To express this tragedy in words seems to draw from me what little bit of strength I have, but I must continue."

My hurt and destruction comes from my son Bobby, better known to the public as Dragon Slyer the He-Man and my daughter Theresa the world renowned concert singer. My daughter Theresa was not only a talented singer, she was a gifted singer. Her voice was immortal and she could take any song and make it beautiful. There were many composers who wrote songs for her to sing, but after the song was performed, it would always be her voice that made the difference. The sound of her voice would be what people would remember. Theresa was becoming depressed and obsessed with finding that special song. She wanted an immortal song to sing with her immortal one of a kind voice. It seems that no composer or song could fit the bill and she traveled near and far in her pursuit. She even went as far as to offer a reward of $100,000.00 cash upfront plus royalties for anyone who was gifted enough to write that special song. Theresa wanted a song that would always be her song and no one ever could sing it the way in which she did. She wanted her voice and that special song to last after she was dead and buried. Then, there was my son Bobby, Dragon Slayer The He- Man. He stood six feet two inches and had the perfect body. Bobby's weight was three hundred pounds of solid muscles and he perfected his body without the use of steroids. He was the picture of health. In the ring, he was number one and never defeated. Bobby brought tremendous honor to the name Mason in the professional wrestling world. The best wrestlers in the world would pour into our training camps in hopes ofbeing like Bobby. Our training camps were expensive and only the best were accepted. Bobby not only was the world champion, but he also held the title for Me Universe. We were very close and when we talked he would always listen with respect.

"They were my only two kids and I loved them with all of my heart, but most of all, they loved me too." Lester was saying as he began to break down again with tears and saliva running from his face.

"You are doing fine," Jeff Wielder said while offering Lester a silk handkerchief. It's ok. to take your time or to pause when necessary, for we are all with you,"Jeff continued.

"Yes, I know that Jeff, and believe me I have to draw strength from time to time, for I am truly a broken man, "Lester said confessingly.

Lester began to explain, "I will finish all that I have to say, but forgive me if I stop many times along the way my friends.

The rest of Lester's closely bonded friends began to put their hands together in applause to show their support and to let him know there was strength there for him to draw from.

"As I was saying, Lester continued, I loved my kids and life was more than sweet. But one day, our lives were to be changed. The change began with my daughter Theresa. A special song that possessed immortality had been written for my daughter. The song, words and lyrics were heart touching. It was the most beautiful and meaningful song that the world had yet to hear. I've asked myself hundreds of times how can something so beautiful and innocent be written by someone so evil, T.P. had written that special song. With that song he won the love of my daughter, Theresa. T.P. gave notice to Theresa's agent of his accomplishment and insisted on only releasing it to her. Theresa's agent raved highly to her about the song and they were to meet in the studio that same night. The three of them were to meet at 7 p.m., but the eagerness of my daughter prompted her to be there at 6 p.m.

She wanted to know more about the song and the writer from her agent. Theresa's agent told her that the song was all that she had been searching for, but the writer had an unusual air about him. Her agent told of T.P.'s atmosphere as best he could, but explained it's something that she would have to experience to really know what he meant. My daughter's agent whose name is Keith, also said that T.P. was quite handsome.

An hour had passed and Theresa and Keith heard the door open and felt the flow of a shiverous breeze that began to gently flow through the studio. As the footsteps began to come closer, Theresa's anticipation began to soar. Suddenly, T.P. turned the corner and faced Theresa with a warm smile and a handsome picture perfect face. Theresa told me that it was love at first sight, but I knew T.P. was incapable love. From that moment on T.P. used his breath taking charm and combined with his looks, his obvious atmosphere was irrelevant to Theresa. My daughter looked over the song that he had written and knew that her search had ended. She had not only found her immortal song but had also found love. She told T.P. that he could pick up his one hundred thousand dollar check and sign the royalty contract the next night over dinner. Theresa gave T.P. a formal invitation to dinner at my mansion. She was eager for T.P. to meet me. Later, that night she told Bobby and myself of T.P. and his immortal song. I immediately warned her of all that I knew of T.P., but I couldn't back up a single word with solid proof. Everything I said was pure speculation. Even though I couldn't prove anything I had said, I knew T.P. was no good, particularly for my daughter. The more I talked against T.P., the stronger Theresa was bonding with him. It got to the point where for the first time in her life, my daughter told me to stay out of this matter, for my words have no more meaning. I was hurt and devastated I then told her that I don't approve of her having any dealings with T.P. and I will say no more. This was the beginning of T.P.'s breakdown of my family. But still, I left with a lot more to say and I had to tell someone, so

I pulled Bobby to the side. I told him all I knew about T.P. and Bobby took all I said to heart. I stressed to him the importance of keeping Theresa safe.

The next morning at breakfast I told Theresa that I couldn't stop her from seeing or dealing with T.P. But I forbid her to see him here in my home. Theresa told me she would honor my will but she is going to see more of him. She made it clear that she was going to see T.P. tonight as planned, but instead of here at the mansion, it would be at a restaurant named Chantals. Theresa gave me the option to attend if I was to change my mind. This was out of the question. I wanted Theresa to know how strong I felt against this, so there was no way in hell that I was going to be there. However, this did not apply to Bobby. I secretly urged him to be there and oversee for Theresa's benefit. I told Bobby to be very discreet about his true purpose for being there. Bobby informed Theresa that he would accompany her to the dinner engagement. At 6:50 p.m., Bobby and Theresa were seated at Chantal's Restaurant awaiting T.P.'s arrival. T.P. entered the restaurant at exactly 7 p.m. and joined Bobby and Theresa at their table. Theresa T.P. to Bobby and there were no gestures of speech. The two of them simply nodded their heads. Theresa had already been made aware of Bobby's attitude by conversation prior to T.P.'s arrival.

After each had ordered their meal, they were served a white wine awaiting the food. Theresa began to speak, "I really appreciate the song that you have written for me. It must have taken lots of time and surely, you must have put your heart and soul in it." "Yes," T.P. replied, in the song I have put much, but my heart and soul is for another. I feel a lot of unexplainable feelings for you and I have followed your career most faithfully. Theresa spoke softly as she blushed, "Even your words are kind and sweet like your song, but if your heart is for another shouldn't you choose your words to me more carefully." "No Theresa," T.P. replied, for I have longed to say kind words to you in hopes of satisfying my inner feelings. It's you that my heart belongs to and I fear that if I don't speak now, I may never get this chance again.

"Enough of this rubbish," Bobby blurted out. Pay him for the song and let him sign the contract, so he can be on his way.

"Don't be rude Bobby," Theresa said firmly. "If anyone is to be on their way, then Bobby it will be you."

I'm not here to cause conflict T.P. quietly spoke, but only to give you my song Theresa and I declined taking money and royalties. This song I have written is full of my affection for you and to take money payment would cheapen my sincerity. I have written this not for money, but only for you.

Before Theresa could respond, Bobby voiced his inner feelings. Let me put it this way. I don't want you to associate with my sister again. Her last name is Mason which means more than you would ever amount to. Our family name is distinguished and has worldwide honor. For the last time be on your way.

T.P. turned to Theresa while saying, "The words Bobby has spoken are for your mouth only, does he speak for you?

Theresa quickly replied, "No, I don't want you to leave.

Bobby seemingly lost control and threw the wine from his glass into the face of T.P. who was still seated. Bobby then stood up and said, "Don't let me have to tell you to leave again.

Theresa shouted, "Bobby what's gotten into you? You have embarrassed me and my guest."

"It's best that I leave now, T.P. said as the doors to the restaurant blew wide open and the night wind swept through the restaurant. Table settings were disrupted and glasses of beverages were overturned on each table. The waitress quickly closed the doors only to leave a drafty atmosphere throughout the restaurant.

T.P. began to rise to his feet as he patted dry his face with the cloth napkins. He stared Bobby in the eyes and with a softly spoken voice said, "Bobby I am sure the day will come when I find great pleasure in meeting you." T.P. excused himself from the table and began to leave when Theresa began to follow him. "T.P. I am sorry for what happened tonight," Theresa told T.P. while clutching his arm and looking remorsed.

T.P. replied, "You have done nothing wrong to be sorry for. On the last page of your song is a number where I can be reached if ever you so desire, but I must go." T.P. turned and slowly left the restaurant never looking back.

Theresa stormed back to the table and retrieved her song and other belongings. She gave Bobby andicy look and told him for this she would never for give, then proceeded to leave.

Later that night, Bobby informed me of all that had transpired at dinner. Even though Bobby was quite capable of taking care of himself and was number one in the world, I feared deeply for his safety, Lester said with his voice fading.

Lester began to loosen his black tie and continue on. "The very next day, a beautiful woman approached Bobby at the center for our training camps and presented him with some pleasing news. She introduced herself as Karen Smith, a freelance agent for film and videos. Karen made Bobby aware of her interest in doing a motion picture about him and his accomplishments. Karen told Bobby, "You are a world renowned superstar with all the right ingredients for making a motion picture a box office hit. Bobby your name alone will sale millions.

Bobby replied, "You're not so bad yourself. When do we start?"

Karen smiled as she spoke, "First, we may start with dinner tonight. I am staying at the Royal Throne. It has fabulous food and I can explain to you about how all of this works."

While flexing his muscles, Bobby began to speak, "My time is committed to day until six p.m. After that the night can be yours.

Karen while using body language told Bobby, "I'll try not to take up too much of your time, so would seven p.m. be convenient for you?"

My son agreed to meet with Karen at seven p.m. in the Royal Throne Restaurant, Lester continued while coughing as if he had swallowed something incorrectly.

Bobby immediately called me on the phone and told me of his good fortune. He expressed how being a movie star seem to intrigue him, but most of all he told of Karen's beauty and refinement. My talk with Bobby was brief because there were other people that he wanted to share his good news with. I was happy for Bobby and I began to think shouldn't I be equally as happy for Theresa whom just had her dream song written? Yes, I should so I began to some what ease up. I told Theresa how happy I was for her and I would try to be a little more understanding. After all, the love for my family was tremendous.

Lester began to become fidgety with his hands and everyone knew that soon he would be voicing the core of his destruction.

Jeff Wielder ordered his butler to refill all glasses as he spoke out. "Lester you are doing fine and you show a brilliant display of courage. Let this toast be for you Lester."

All of the men rose to their feet and stood like knights in armor as they out their glasses together in tribute.

Lester smiled a painful smile and with eyes that watered his cheeks, began to continue. "The words that I had spoken to Theresa seemed to lift her spirits and she gave me a tender embrace. Theresa adjourned to the parlor and began to use the phone. She was calling T.P. and making dinner arrangement once more. They were to be private, one on one. I made myself distant from the parlor and went for a walk in the courtyard.

As time passed and the evening rolled around, Bobby was making his way to the Royal Throne. Bobby and Karen were enjoying their meal and each other's company when Bobby spoke to Karen. "Tell me more about the movie deal."

Karen began to smile as she stared into Bobby's sparkling eyes. "Yes, Bobby, I should be going over this with you, but somehow I seem to have gotten caught up in this moment. Please forgive me," Karen asked.

Bobby told Karen that it was perfectly O.K. for he too felt magic in the air. The way Karen explained, the procedures were simple and clear. There was to be a two part agreement. The first part consisted of a movie relapse form that gave the funders of the movie the right to release and show the movie for the receptive of capital invested, plus profits. On the form was the title of the movie which would be Mason's House of Champions, starring Bobby Dragon Slayer, The He-Man and the release agreement. Karen expressed, "This form must be signed and delivered before any capital can be advanced for production. Once you sign the release form, I will give you two scripts to read over and upon acceptance of one by you, the negotiation of the contract would be next. These people are very liberal when it comes to what they want, so I assure you of a good contract. Once that is signed, we will start production. I have the release agreement in my room so if you are really interested, you need only sign it and I will take a flight out tomorrow and return two days from now with two scripts.

"My son assured Karen that there would be no problem in him signing the release agreement. Bobby told me how he and Karen danced the night away and it was like floating on a cloud. As time passed and the night grew later, Bobby and Karen ended it up in Karen's hotel room. Bobby, after a few more drinks of white wine, signed the release form to start the ball rolling. He told me there was no sex but a strong maybe when she returned in two days. The next day Karen was to leave and deliver the movie release.

Please try to follow me closely on what I am telling you guys, because I have two hurts brewing at the same time," Lester said as he wiped his forehead. Theresa and T.P. were only blocks away at a restaurant called Starburst. They too were having a joyful romantic evening. They discussed the recording of Theresa's song and she was becoming overwhelmed and overpowered by T.P.'s charm. Their night ended up at T.P.'s penthouse," cried out Lester with all the tears and wrinkles his face could bare. It was like T.P. had taken her mind, soul and body. The next day I overheard her on the house phone with one her closet girlfriends, telling how she can still feel T.P. moving inside her body. Theresa's two hour phone conversation was totally about T.P. I felt helpless, but she was so overjoyed. She began the recording of her immortal song and demanded that T.P. must be at her side. Time was passing and still there was no immediate danger or signs of terror in my life. I found myself beginning to live day by day. I just couldn't bring myself to feel good about T.P. no matter how hard I tried.

Two days had passed and once more Bobby was approached by Karen at the training center. grabbed Karen and picked her up in the air while turning her body around in a circle. He acted as though the two of them were long lost lovers. Karen told Bobby that she had two scripts for him to read over Bobby insisted that she give him the scripts over dinner. Karen agreed, "The time and place will be the same as last time." Bobby came home and I could feel the joy bubbling over inside of him. He was so happy and thrilled, but I think mostly, it was Karen's return. Later on that night, Bobby and Karen had their candlelit dinner. It was a wine and roses occasion, with music in the air. At night's end Bobby and Karen found themselves in Karen's suite and Bobby was given all that his heart desired. He left the next morning with two scripts, for Bobby, it seemed that there was love everywhere. He was so full of life and excitement. However, Bobby was told he had two weeks to look over the scripts for his approval. The next two weeks Bobby and Karen were inseparable. This was also the case for Theresa and T.P. Portions of each day and night after night, T.P. and Theresa shared themselves in total lust. I was quickly losing my daughter to T.P. at an accelerated rate. By the end of two weeks, Theresa totally belonged to T.P. Theresa's immortal song instantly soared to the top of the charts and after two weeks it was number one in six countries.

There was so much joy and love in the air that two weeks has past, barely noticed. Karen wanted Bobby to give his approval or disapproval of the scripts for her backers were awaiting his decision. Bobby found total satisfaction in both scripts. He felt that each scripted portrayed him and the family with worldwide honor. Karen informed Bobby that he may make his final decision tonight over dinner, but in the meanwhile, she needed him to look at a vacant warehouse that could be transformed into a simulated training camp. One of the scenes called for a training cameo to be burned and destroyed. Bobby agreed and the two of them drove cross town at the address that Karen had on a card. Once Karen and Bobby arrived at the warehouse, the building they saw was in pretty good shape and stood three stories.

Bobby spoke out, "It's a shame to have to burn down such a perfect building."

Karen replied, "Only the front section will burn and Special effects will take it from there. After which it shall be restored. The making of a good movie doesn't come cheap and this particular movie is going to cost way too much.

As Bobby began to shake his head, he said, "It still seem such a waste."

Come Bobby, I need you to come inside. This is where your expertise will be needed.

My son and Karen began to enter the building through a side door that was unlocked. Karen explained to Bobby that on each floor of the warehouse is suppose to be a separate training camp. Karen wanted Bobby to start with the third floor and work his way down. She insisted that each floor will be set up the way he felt was right. Karen and Bobby began to climb the dirty stairs, moving cobwebs and spiders along the way. Once reaching the third floor, Bobby looked around and said, "It's not going to be too bad."

Suddenly another voice spoke out, "Its worst then you think and its going to get much worst." Karen and Bobby turned quickly to see who had spoken those words. Standing before him was a man dressed in a solid red jogging suit with a red stocking - like hooded mask over his face.

"Who are you?" Bobby shouted as he watched the stranger begin to come towards him.

"I am the horse that can't be rode and the man that can't be thrown. I am the master of the game and I am going to destroy you and the name Mason for one thousand years." The stranger spoke in a cold voice.

The night wind began to howl as it entered the building through broken window panes and swept across the floor, clearing a path free of trash and debris.

Bobby and the stranger stood only ten feet apart when Karen pulled from her tote bag a camcorder and began to record what was to take place.

Bobby looked at Karen and chock covered his face as he spoke, "Karen, you are nothing but a cheap whore and after I'm done with him, I'll make you wish you were never born! No one fucks with a Mason.

"There is no after for you Bobby, there is only this time and it's for one thousand years, the stranger spoke as he leaped six to seven feet in the air while launching two lightening fast kicks.

Bobby caught the right foot of the stranger with both hands that could easily bench press five hundred pounds. It was the second kick and the left foot of the stranger that broke Bobby's jaw and sent him sailing across the concrete floor. After having the brick wall to stop Bobby from sailing further, Bobby quickly tried to regroup himself as his mouth hung wide open. Bobby was dazed and the pain of his jaw being broken began to soar. Bobby climbed to his feet, as his mind tried to convince his body that he was still champion of the world. Bobby knew that he had to figure out quickly how to overcome the stranger because the stranger was fast and lethal. The stranger was a born killer that was totally evil. Bobby figured he should make the first move this time. He charged forward in hopes of getting his hands on the stranger's body. As Bobby charged forward with both hands extended and releasing a loud battle cry, the stranger charged forward to meet Bobby while the night wind unleashed a howl of terror. As Bobby reached for the collar and throat of the stranger, the stranger side stepped Bobby and with pinpoint accuracy, launched a lethal blow to Bobby's lower rib cage causing two ribs to be broken and inducing internal hemorrhaging. Bobby dropped to the floor like a ton of bricks. It was over and done with in less than two minutes. Bobby's body was full of pain and any kind of moving was unbearable. The world champion had no chance and was dethroned. The stranger slowly walked over to Bobby and snatched him to his feet by his arm, while twisting his arm one hundred eighty degrees. He then walked Bobby over to a steel ballinster and with a lightening chop, broke Bobby's twisted arm at the elbow. Bobby's body was full of pain and torment as his broken jaw muffled his scream. The stranger draped Bobby's broken and busted body over the steel ballinster, while handcuffing his hands to his feet. Bobby was bent and cuffed over the steel ballinster like a bent horseshoe. Karen began to move in closer with the camcorder as the stranger snatched Bobby's hair to raise his head. The stranger told Bobby that the World Championship Title will go to another and the name Mason, I will put to shame for generations to come. The stranger then pushed Bobby's face back down against the steel railings causing blood from Bobby's nose to squirt and drip to the second floor. The stranger then dropped Bobby's pants and shorts to his knees and fucked him two times while Bobby, my son screamed and mourned. His body bled inside and outside as he experienced his manhood and family name being taken away and totally destroyed. After the stranger finished with Bobby, he told him that the movie rights belonged to him, but Bobby could write a book entitled Mason's House of Drag. The stranger then placed a 9mm pistol and one bullet in Bobby's pocket and told him the gun is for company, for on your way to the hospital, the ambulance can be a lonely place. The stranger and Karen then left the building and left Bobby cuffed and totally destroyed. The paramedics were notified and came to Bobby's aide only minutes later. They loaded Bobby into the ambulance and before one of the paramedics could get inside with Bobby and close the door, there was a gunshot. Bobby had killed himself. His head was totally destroyed. The next night I received a copy of the video and I died a thousand deaths, Lester said as he grabbed his chest and stumbled back to his chair. Everyone rushed to Lester' side to give aide or emergency help.

Lester said, while looking flushed and pale interchangeably, "In my pocket are my pills, help me please."

"I have them Lester," Jermaine said quickly. Lester quickly stuck the pill beneath his tongue and began to take deep breathes.

"Just relax Lester, we all know your grief runs deep. You need not go on," Jeff said while patting Lester's forehead. Lester took for himself a couple of minutes and began to lean forward.

"I'll be fine dear friends," Lester said. "Even if it kills me, I must finish the game. The same gun that T.P. gave Bobby is the same gun that's located in the glove compartment of his car. The gun and the one bullet was my contribution to T.P.'s birthday celebration," Lester said as he began to laugh with tears rolling into his mouth.

Everyone joined in with laughter and gratitude.

"As I was saying, "Lester continued, "T.P. was still not done with destruction. On the same day I received a copy of the video, Karen was found murdered in a hotel called Slept Inn.

She had been strangled with some kind of fine wire. Karen was the only link to the mask killer that the police investigation had to go on. The investigator questioned the desk clerk and found that Karen had only one visitor that they knew of. He was a man named Carl Simpson, head of Simpson's Video Production. When the police questioned him, he told of a prearranged meeting with Karen. Carl told how he solicited for the purpose of buying Karen's video and movie release rights. Karen had told him to come to her suite and view the video and if he was interested, he would have two hours to bring one million dollars in cash back to the suite. As far as Carl knew, there were three other producers that had the same deal and the video would be sold on a first come first serve basis. Carl told police that the video was a gold mine and he immediately put the cash together and returned to the hotel. Carl purchased the video and movie release rights for one million dollars cash. He said he last saw Karen alive at 2 p.m. The killer made sure Carl would be in the clear to exploit the video through out the world. At 2:30p.m., Karen called room service and ordered champagne. When the bell boy brought the champagne, Karen gave him a fifty dollar tip and asked him for the correct time, which as 2:35 p.m. Therefore, Carl could not have been Karen's murderer and to buy and show the video worldwide was legal. The police concluded that Karen's murderer was the mask man in the video. They believed he entered and exited Karen's suite from the fire escape which lead to a side alley. Everything came to halt. The police didn't know who to look for or where to look. Even if they obtained the killer, there was no way it could be proven unless the killer confessed to it himself. The name Mason was put to shame all over the world. I had to close down all training camps because everyone turned away. No one wanted to be a part of Mason House of Champions anymore. The family name was the laughing stock of the world. I had Bobby's funeral closed to the public, for private reasons, not because everyone wanted to come. Due to the condition of

Bobby's face the coffin could not be opened. At the funeral, I took an oath of revenge to see T.P. die at my hand. I knew this day would come and it was for this day that I've lived," Lester said in an angry sobbing voice.

Theresa was hurt by Bobby's death and the family honor being destroyed, but not like I felt she should be. She was lost to T.P. and all of his illusions of love. It was soon after Bobby's death that Theresa announced her wedding plans to me. Theresa told me that she and T.P. were to be married quickly and quietly. Theresa also informed me that she was two months pregnant. I was outraged. My daughter was marrying the bastard that brought death and shame to our family. As much as I wanted to say, I could only say nothing. Theresa was too far gone and to deeply lost in T.P. She would only rebel and pull further from me if I dared to speak against T.P., for T.P. in her eyes could do no wrong. So, I had to bite the bullet and bide my time and not let them know how I really felt, for T.P. was far too dangerous to go heads up with. But deep in my heart, I knew that T.P. must be destroyed by my hands and I knew Theresa must not bring his devil child into this world. The solution to my problem must be found in three weeks, for Theresa and T.P. were to be married in Florida at that time. I was worth billions, but Theresa alone was worth only about fifty million. I felt sure that T.P. was after the combined wealth of the both of us. If T.P. married Theresa then my daughter and I would be marked for death. I had to do something and it had to be fast. After having to shut down all of my training camps, losing franchises and sports contracts due to Bobby's death and the bad publicity. I told Theresa and T.P. that all of my assets had been frozen. I informed them that I was becoming financially destroyed as well. I knew that T.P. didn't just seek wealth, he sought power as well. He wanted to rule the world and for this it takes billions of dollars. I figured that T.P. might back off Theresa after reevaluating the monetary wealth that's to be gained. After T.P. would dump Theresa, then I felt that I could persuade her to have and abortion and make her see T.P. for what he really was. Due to the fact that Bobby and Theresa had legal rights to Mason's enterprises, there were many legal documents that both of them had to sign for profit sharing reasons. I used this to my advantage, Lester continued on.

I had my lawyer freeze all of Theresa's monetary accounts and assets in a legal manner that didn't point the finger back to me. My lawyer made it seem like standard procedure which is truly done in a case such as mine. After all, all my investments were failing and being closed down. Nevertheless, this was the iron in the fire that became hot and began to glow. Theresa was evicted out of T.P.'s penthouse and returned to the mansion. She was heart broken and devastated. She told me T.P. had all her belongings sent over to the studio where she was recording. Theresa was given a note by the driver that tore her apart and destroyed her will to live. The note simply read No More Never. The thrill is gone.

My plan was successful but it destroyed my daughter. Day after day, my daughter would sit and rock in a chair and never spoke. Theresa wouldn't even exchange pleasantries. For three days she didn't eat nor drink. I called for my private doctor and he admitted her to the hospital. While feeding her intravenously and running test, the doctor told me Theresa would be dead in four days. When the doctor told me that I lost all my senses and began to grab him while screaming No! NO! The orderlies and nurse had to restrain me and the doctor administered me a sedative. Later, after I was clam, the doctor returned to finish explaining.

He told me there were multiple reasons why Theresa was dying. The first was because of the baby. The baby's system was too different from that of Theresa. Theresa was being drained of her body's necessities and her cellular structures were breaking down at an accelerated pace. At the rate of the baby's growth, Theresa would have to eat six well balanced meals a days plus take an assortment of vitamins. If Theresa was to do that then she would live for four months. She would then die on the delivery table giving birth. It would be a super healthy baby born in only six months but it would take the life of Theresa. The second reason is Theresa has no will to live. She has no will at all. The doctor told men that if and only if Theresa had a strong will and ate six meals a day stay on IVs and be confined in the hospital for the next four months would she live long enough to give birth. But without the strong will and the cooperation of Theresa eating, there is nothing that can be done. The baby will draw from Theresa ten times what the IV feeding will give. The doctor told me he was sorry but he had never seen or experienced nothing like this before. I thought why not do an abortion, and that way Theresa still may live. The doctor then told me if he did an abortion, it would mean instant death. Theresa knew nothing of this, but she seems to wait for death to come. "I spent the last four days of Theresa's life by her side, watching her body deteriorate to nothing but skin and bones,"Lester said as he cried and wimped. My daughter died of a broken heart while the evil seed of T.P. sucked the life from her. When she died, I had that evil seed removed from her body and her body cremated.

"So there you are my friends. This is all that's left of what was a powerful proud man. T.P. left me with a destroyed life, no family and a name full of shame and dishonor," Lester said as he fell to the floor face down.

Everyone came to Lester's rescue and helped him to a comfortable chair. Once more a pill was placed beneath Lester's tongue and he drew strength from the bond of his friends, which now was not in abundance as before. Lester's story had taken its toll on all, but the tightly bonded men cling together to go on and finish the game.

"Let's all rise and toast Lester," David said while drying his eyes with the wrist of his hands, "Lester, you have slain a mighty dragon by enduring what has happened to you. I am proud to know you and call you friend. This toast is to your honor and you have the respect of all of us here, for this bond shall not be broken nor tarnished by no man."

After hearing David speak with such conviction and commitment. The men once more put their hands together in applause.

As Lester slowly stood up from his chair, he began to speak, "Tonight I have survived my tragedy once more, but this time, the burden of it all seems just a little lighter. To voice the hurt and share its pain among friends who can identify is truly the only way."

"Yes", the fifth and final guest by the name of Henry Sites spoke. "I too must rid my soul of the hurt and bitter pains of T.P.'s death and destruction. I am the last to finish the game and with the strength of our bond, I shall do so."

"We are all with you Henry, so you may turn to us and draw as much strength as you may require," Jeff spoke as he looked at the Rolex on his wrist.

"Even though we all agreed that T.P. should die a horrible death alone with no one to call out for help, I really would like to see the look on his face right about now, Jermaine said while laughing. "No," Henry spoke out. "To die even among enemies has its dignity. T.P. must die alone like a stray dog and he must have no one to hear his last words. We shall dispose of him like a toilet disposes of unwanted valueless waste."

"Agreed! Agreed! Agreed!," the men of the bond began to speak out as they clapped their hands together.

"Let us drink plenty, for tonight we shall cool down T.P.'s burnt remains with a long and satisfying piss." Jeff spoke with a trembling smile on his face.

"Yes! Yes! We should drink all the way to the piss site and soak him down good." Lester said while breathing deeply.

"So we shall," Jeff spoke out. "My limo stays stocked with the best pissing beverage made." Everyone began to laugh for with the pain that they suffered, a light side of humor was not only needed but well deserved.

"I have a question to ask that has always puzzled me and maybe you can answer it for me Jeff," David said while pouring down more champagne.

"If I know the answer, I will be more then glad to enlighten you David," Jeff blurted out.

"I know T.P. was given the last name of Wielder by you, but what does T.P. stand for?" David asked with a puzzled looked on his face.

"I can only tell you of T.P.'s five last names given to him by his foster parents. His first name has always been simply T.P. "However, I've asked the same question of T.P. and sought to find out if he desired another first name," Jeff explained as he continued on. "T.P. told me his initials stand for Total Package and it shall never be changed. Not now, not ever and by no man. We never had that conversation again."

"I see," David said, "But what the hell, that bastard will have neither marker or grave."

"I know he should be burned and blown into many parts, but how should we totally dispose of his burnt pissed on remains? David asked.

"I was saving that for a surprise, "Jeff said as he smiled. But I might as well tell you all now. I will have my servants put his remains in the sewer near the waste treatment plant on the north road."

Everyone stood and applauded Jeff's surprise with faces of a joyful hurt.

CHAPTER SEVEN

"**W**ELL I GUESS IT'S TIME to finish the game and relieve my suffering", Henry said as he walked slowly to the center of the floor. "I too was a rich and powerful man who had a good life, a loving wife and two wonderful daughters. But my friends, what I am about to say comes hard, but it will answer your questions and give a total picture of T.P. and his evil. The things I say will be finishing pieces to the puzzle. To begin, I must take everyone back to the time in my life before T.P. was found in the trash can. I came from a family of old money and being an only child, I had the world at my feet. I was interested in religious research. My time was spent trying to find the truth of man's existence. Some how, I wanted to be close to God in a manner in which he would speak to me as he spoke to man in the days of old. This was to be my life long quest and my shining star. My wife was a perfect match for me. She totally believed in God and she was raised to be pure in heart. My wife's name was Monica and she maintained her virginity until our wedding night. It was so romantic and well worth the wait for. To be part of a first time is something that one never forgets, whether it may be good or bad. But ours was mystical." Henry said with a bitter smile on his face. Monica and I were living a life made in heaven, and our thrust for knowledge was becoming intensely beautiful. I believed that no matter how bad or good people and things were, it was not by accident or because something went wrong. For example, Lucifer was supposed to be the most beautiful of all angels and possess more of what angels are made of. Some kind of way this perfect angel became corrupt and evil was then casted from heaven. All of the bad, suffering, hatred, disease and sickness throughout the world is suppose to come from Lucifer. God is given credit for all that is good and Lucifer is given credit for all that is bad." Henry was saying when interrupted by David.

"Yes!" this is true and the evil bastard T.P. is an example of Lucifer's evil, David blurted out.

"Not so fast David," please hear me out Henry continued. "The God Almighty does not make mistakes or errors. He doesn't create people, things, angels and they turn out wrong or not like expected. God is Almighty and far beyond man's comprehension. But most of all, God's creations are all perfect. There are no flaws, mistakes or errors. By that I mean this, God created Lucifer to be evil as can be. We are talking 100% evil with power and mind of a superior being far greater than man He's not nor will be on the level equal to God, but he is on the level in which he was created. Lucifer is an angel that has superiority from that position down to man. Lucifer was created for the sole purpose of giving man a choice. Before Lucifer, there was only a world of good, free from sin, and there were no choices to choose from. In order for man to choose, there must be good and evil in existence. This my friends is why Lucifer was created by God Almighty and it was no mistake. Lucifer is doing the job that God ordained him to do. Lucifer was created to be totally evil with no trace of decency. As you have seen and experienced, Lucifer does his job quite well. Bare with me my friends while I give you this short sermon which has taken me years to learn. This will give you all insight on how this evil bastard T.P. functions and help you understand the total picture of him, Henry continued.

Lucifer is mighty, but with all the powers that he possesses, he does not have the power to give life. He can only possess a life which God had given, but at the same token, Lucifer can enter that life at anytime to make it sin and do evil depending on the inner strength of that person. This person would become bad hut not totally bad and stand a chance to recover depending on how strong the good is in that person and the desire to do what is right. Plus my friend, each one of us has a chance to ask for forgiveness from all that we've done wrong, which saves us from Lucifer's clutch.

"O.K., stay with me my friends, for I am almost there where I can begin to finish the game, Henry talked on. Now we have right and wrong which gives man the choice, but there is one loop hole." Man can say, "How can God expect me to do right when one of his angels couldn't do right, for I am only a mortal man. Man would be justified in saying that and might could get by with it providing he was ignorant of the fact why Lucifer was created. God showed man that it can be done and no excuses will be tolerated. God sent his only son down to earth to be born of mortal flesh. His name was called Jesus. Jesus saw and felt the same things that we mortal men saw and felt, but he kept the faith and chose right over wrong. In the end, he lived the life of a poor man and died the worst death possible, which was crucifixion. Crucifixion is when nails are driven through your wrist and feet on a cross and you hang like that while the sun bakes your bleeding body until your heart pumps air. Then you die. So, Jesus' purpose was to show mankind that God's will can be done by mortal man. Therefore, man can offer no excuse for his short comings. Now my friends, Lucifer has done the same thing but with a completely opposite purpose. Lucifer seeded a fertile egg in the womb of my late wife Monica and a bastard that was totally evil was born. He was T.P. Henry cried out as he balled up his fists and began to shake and tremble.

All of the men rose up to their feet and wore faces of shock as they rushed to the aide of Henry. As they put their arms around Henry in comfort, they all began to ask questions.

Henry are you T.P.'s father, David shouted. "NO! NO!, HELL NO! "Henry replied as he continued to talk. Everybody settle down I'll be fine, It's just so much I have to explain in sharing my hurt. I must finish the game my friends so please bare with me.

As I was saying, my wife Monica and I had a lovely marriage and our goals were pretty much the same. The both of us continued our religious research for the next three years, which were good years. We became the proud parents of two beautiful daughters. Their names were Stella and Belinda. They were kind, sensitive and sweet children. Stella and Belinda meant the world to me and my wife. Monica and I raised them to be lovingly and filled their lives full of the love of God. The next year I decided to take my family to Jerusalem to visit the holy land and I wanted to further my religious research. We were in the country for about six months when our lives were to be changed. Monica and I were doing research while holding religious seminars. Everyone knew Monica and me as we prowled the country with our research and lectures. We began to have a great following of people from all walks of life. We really felt good about ourselves, for we were teaching and learning at the same time. One night while giving a seminar, a tall stranger entered the room dressed in a black hooded robe. He had long curly red hair and a long red beard, his eyes had the look of tombstones, but most of all, he possessed a cold windy atmosphere. The stranger stood in the rear of the room with his head bowed. It was only a matter of minutes before the room was completely empty, excluding my family and the stranger. About two hundred people had vacated the seminar without a word being spoken. The stranger then approached the front of the room and gave us three days to leave the country. I asked him by what right does he have to order us to leave. The only reply was "Zola has spoken and I will never tell you again." The stranger then left and with him went the cold drafty atmosphere.

My family and I were upset about what had happened and all of us knew he was no ordinary man. But nevertheless I refused to be pushed around by the stranger, for I too was a powerful man in the world. I began the next day inquiring about who Zola was and what made him different. I was told by many that he was an evil man who possessed great powers. Zola was known throughout Jerusalem for his demonic powers. After discussing the matter over with my family, we agreed we should leave for safety reason. But instead of leaving in three days as ordered by Zola, I chose to leave on the fifth day. I wanted to hold one more seminar as a show of strength. Out of fear for my family, I hired four armed body guards for protection. The fourth night, Monica and my two daughters remained at the hotel with two of the body guards. I was to go to the seminar with the remaining two guards. At the seminar, there were only a handful of participants and after forty five minutes had past,they too began to leave. I returned to the hotel with my bodyguards and found no one at the front desk, I could feel the drafty atmosphere and the presence of Zola. I quickly charged up the stairs to my room only to see Zola coming out. My bodyguards quickly pulled their 9mm while Zola did the same. It was a fierce exchange of gunshots, but after it was over, one body guard laid face down on the floor dead with multiple gunshot wounds. My second bodyguard was still tumbling down the stairs to his death and I was on my knees from a gun shot wound to my right shoulder. Zola was still standing with multiple wounds to his chest and neck. There was a big crack of thunder and a sharp flash of lightening. As Zola fell dead on the floor. "I rose to my feet and rushed into our hotel room and found my wife badly beaten and half naked, I grabbed Monica with my one good arm and held her tightly against my chest. She quickly informed me that she had been raped by that evil man. In the corner of the room were my two daughters. They were terrified. The evil bastard made them stay in the corner of the room and watch, "Henry explained while his eyes ran water and his body trembled.

The closely bonded friends of Henry rushed to hi side and all wanted to put their arms around him. They knew his boundaries of hurt and pain may have no limits.

"Take a few minutes for yourself Henry, we will travel this road of terror and pain with you, "Jermaine said in a soft voice.

"Yes, pace yourself as need be Henry, we're all for one here tonight.", Jeff agreed.

"Thank you my friends. No you all are much more than friends. The bond that we have formed tonight, I call it family, Henry said with gratitude.

"Let's refill our glasses, for I know no worthier toast, Jeff said as he rose to his feet.

Each of the men stood and placed one of their hands on top of the other as they bumped their champagne glasses together and chanted the family, the family,

"I must go on my brothers, so please stay with me on what I say. My strength is in short supply," Henry explained as he separated himself from his friends in order to continue on. It was only four days later when my wife grew ill ad we found out that she was pregnant. Monica had to be hospitalized immediately, so our trip back to the states had to be postponed. The doctors told me the identical terms that Lester had to face pertaining to his daughter Theresa, God rest her soul. Monica had to be confined to the hospital for the next six months while her body was being pumped with food and wonder drugs. Our faith didn't allow abortion procedure, so we agreed for Monica to have the child and then I would put it up for adoption. My daughters and I were at Monica's side everyday for the next six months. We mourned and grieved among ourselves but we tried to show hope and cheer at Monica's bedside. Through all parts of the day and night, my daughters and I would pray for a healing miracle. The next six months in Jerusalem seemed to pass so very quickly. Monica was being rushed to the delivery room to give birth and to die. I stood their holding Monica's hand and caressing her forehead while feeling so helpless, I was wishing I could die in her place. Monica screamed four short screams and as the doctor pulled the baby from Monica's womb, I could feel the body temperature in her hand and forehand begin to drop rapidly. Their was no after birth or umbilical cord to cut but yet it was the most beautiful baby that I had ever seen. The doctors were astonished with shock as they raised the baby for Monica to view. As the baby opened its eyes and looked at Monica there was a heavy roar of thunder and a flash of lightening. The shutters on the windows began to clatter and the wind outside began to howl like trumpets. The baby never cried or uttered a word. Monica gently squeezed my hand and closed her eyes for the very last time. My beloved wife was no more the doctors admitted me for an overnight stay and gave me tranquilizers. My two daughters and I left the country with, my wife's body and the baby two days later. I decided to put it up for adoption in the states. Somehow I felt that maybe the part of Monica that was in the baby might make a difference. Monica was so pure and trustworthy. It was that reason which made my decision so difficult.

We all arrived in New York and my limo was waiting for us at the airport. My daughters and I were transported to the mansion and my wife's body was picked up by my funeral director. The funeral was sad and heart breaking for me, but it was especially hard for Stella and Belinda. They worshipped the ground their mother walked upon. Two days after Monica's funeral, I was going over a pamphlet on the adoption process and how it worked. The baby was now about ten days old and something strange occurred that changed my mind totally about any type of adoption. The ten day old baby was chanting Zola, Zola, Zola. I took one look at the baby and it smiled so innocently at me. I summoned for my limo to take me and the baby into the inner city. I knew that the baby was evil and the fact hat Monica was it's mother wouldn't make a difference. The baby must be destroyed, but my faith would not permit killing in any shape, fashion, or form. I decided to abandon the baby in a trash can in Brooklyn. The baby would suffocate to death or be compressed in the compactor of the truck. Some how I felt the evil would be destroyed and my hands would be washed clean. That was the last time that I saw the baby until it had reached manhood. I was so sure that the baby had perished and died. So my friends, that is how that evil bastard came to existence, "Henry said as he sat down and dropped his head.

"You're doing fine Henry," Jeff spoke as he ordered refills for everybody's glass.

"Thank you Jeff, but I must take a couple of minutes for myself before I continue," Henry explained with a dehydrated look on his tear stained face. "Take as much time as you need," David said as he patted Henry on the shoulder.

None of the men wanted to rush Henry because they knew his story of grief was putting everything in focus. They knew that Henry's pain had been long endured, and finally he may once and for all be able to find some inner peace.

"I must continue on with this and rid my soul of this hurt that I bare, Henry told his friends as he once more began to stand.

"As time passed, I began to watch my young daughters grow into beautiful devoted women. There were never any men in their lives. Stella and Belinda were scared badly by having to watch their mother being raped and the hurt that followed. My daughters were living and working in Australia in a missionary. Stella and Belinda were nuns and enjoying every minute of it. We would often talk for hours on the phone and constantly I would fly to and from Australia to visit them. The three of us were very close and my only regret was that Monica was not living to see the blossoms of our flowers. Life once more was sweet and enjoyable. As time passed, I began to write and publish different religious documentaries. This lead to being guest star on several TV talk shows. Everything was just great. My work was consuming a lot of my idle time and I had the love of Stella and Belinda to comfort me."

One Saturday afternoon, I was sitting in my greenhouse when my butler delivered to me a cable gram. It had been sent from Australia, so I quickly opened it to examine the contents. From that moment on, my entire life took a change for the worst. The cablegram instructed me to be in Australia within two days to negotiate the release of my daughters. I was to be contacted at the monastery at 5 p.m. Monday and given further instructions.

I was in total shock. Drastic events had taken place which I had no knowledge of, so I immediately Sister Lori gave called the monastery in Australia. me a quick briefing on all that had taken place. She told me that Stella and Belinda had been abducted by a stranger dressed in red with a matching hooded mask. The stranger instructed them not to call me because he would notify me personally. Also to show his sincerity, the stranger launched a lethal blow to the throat of Sister Grace which killed her instantly. He then gave Sister Lori a sealed envelope to give me upon arrival. The stranger then instructed Sister Lori that the envelope is for my eyes only and any deviations will not be tolerated. The stranger told Sister Lori that, if his demands were not followed explicitly, then he would return like a thief in the night and leave death and destruction for all to suffer. Sister Lori informed me that the cold evilness of the stranger could be felt by all, so she dared not rise against him. I assured Sister Lori that she must obey him and pray for God's help in the matter. I immediately started packing and preparing my self to take the next available flight out. I had to be in Australia by 5 p.m. Monday for my daughter's sake, Henry cried out as his body shook and trembled.

"Slow yourself down Henry, for your wounds of hurt are severe," Lester spoke out.

"Yes take a minute for yourself, Jeff said while putting his arm around Henry's shoulder.

All of Henry's friends came to his aid to offer him strength and compassion. If Henry, as to finish the game, the men knew that it would take a tremendous supply of inner strength, which at the time was not in abundance. Henry's friends also needed a minute or two in order to regroup and hold there supporting position, for Henry's grief was taking its toll on all.

After recomposing himself, Henry began to continue once more. "While seated on the plane, my mind wouldn't let me have a moment of peace. I knew that terror awaits me and I knew not the condition of my daughters. Stella and Belinda were always kept and raised safely. I protected Stella and Belinda from the evilness of the world, after them baring witness to Monica's tragedy. May time before my plane touched down for landing, my face would fill with tears and my heart would weaken. I was about to go heads up with T.P.'s reign of evil with only my faith and prayers to protect me. The worst part of it all was that it wasn't about money or power. It was personal. The baby that I should have killed at birth has returned to my life with intentions of revenge. I knew the confirmation between T.P. and me would surely end in death, and I must do everything in my power to ensure that it would be his death. I must destroy him once and for all, but I couldn't plan or prepare myself. The mind of T.P. was evil and superior. It was impossible to contemplate what he was going to do and how he was going to do it. T.P. would offer his victims zero chances and options filled with only terror. T.P. was truly the king of predators but somehow along the way, I must find a way to destroy him. The lives of my daughters depended on me doing that. I felt that mankind itself was at stake. During the rest of the flight I decided to pray for strength and guidance. Finally, the plane landed and I quickly summoned a cab to take me toward the monastery. The cab could only go so far, the monastery was deep in the bush. The last twenty miles of the trip has to be made by a four wheel drive vehicle which could be rented at the bordering village. When I arrived at the village, I had to wait, due to the fact that there were only two vehicles and one of them bad been stolen. They later found it deep in the bush destroyed. It was quite obvious to me that this was the work of T.P. The villagers just don't know how lucky they were that no one was near the vehicle when T.P. came for it. I waited for about two hours before the only vehicle returned to the village. After hiring the driver, we quickly set out for the monastery. It was only a twenty mile trip, but the terrain was so thick and brutal that it took two and half hours to reach the monastery. As I walked toward the monastery, I was met by Sister Lori in all her glory. Her face began to frown as her eyes began to release a down pour of tears. She told me to come inside where she would give me the envelope. Sister Lori had faith that all would end well. As I began to open the envelope and read the instructions, the Sister watched my face very closely in hopes of having a clue to its contents.

The note was short and explicit. I was to be at the high plateau by noon tomorrow and come alone. From the high plateau a person could see for miles while remaining undetected. The note offered a threat of death for my daughter if I didn't comply fully. It was about six miles to the plateau and the trip had to be made by mule. At the monastery there were four mules and T.P. had taken two of them. He left one for me to use for my journey which accounted for three. The fourth mule was slain by T.P. It was to be a three hour ride by mule so, I planned to leave at dawn's first light. That night, I ate well and rested my body, but my mind was weary with horrible thoughts. And sleep would not come. At dawn's first light, the sisters had packed enough food for my trip there and hopefully for the trip back. The sisters and I spent forty five minutes in prayer for the safe return of all. They then bid me God speed and I was off on a journey into terror.

I had been traveling the beaten path to the plateau about two hours and I knew my journey would soon be over. The bush was well populated with wildlife creatures and an assortment of blood sucking insects. The air born insects seem to alternate feasting on me and my mule, but the snakes along the way caused me the most trouble, while frightening my mule. The snakes were large and fierce and often I would have to tie my mule and fight them for passage through the bush where detour did not permit. As I traveled further into the bush, I began to detect the smell of something that laid dead and rotten close by. The smell and the baking heat were unbearable, but for my daughters sake I knew that I had to go on. I traveled for another twenty minutes and my eyes beheld what my nose had smelled. The bodies of two of the neighboring tribes laid in the bush beside the trail. They were covered with flies, maggots and scavenger type creatures. The cause of death had to be assumed, but deep in my heart, I knew I was on the right trail and T.P. had traveled this way before me. The last couple of miles to the plateau left me spell bound. I knew not what fate held in store for me nor the situation that I would have to deal with. I only knew that I would be given little or no chance by a man that knew no mercy. The more I thought, the more worried I became. There was so much that I didn't know. I knew not the conditions of my daughters nor what they were going through, but I knew that Stella and Belinda must be totally terrified. Stella and Belinda were all that I lived for. Without them I had nothing, so often and continuously I prayed for their safety. I tried to breathe deeply and flex my muscles while riding the mule in hopes of rejuvenating my self, for I must be alert and my senses sharp if I am to perform at my best. I must be prepared to take the first opportunity presented to destroy T.P., even if I have to lose my life in the process. My daughters must live at all cost, and T.P. must be destroyed at my cost only.

As I neared the plateau I could feel a breeze begin to stir and softly blow. My heart beat began to quicken and I felt like an insect beneath a microscope. The closer I came to the plateau, the more frighten I became. It was as if a small boy was sent to do a man's job. The more I tried to pull myself together, the more my insides would tremble, but I told my self that my daughter's lives I will save. Suddenly, there were flashes of light beaming against my face. I could tell that it was the sun's reflection in a mirror and I was being signaled by that evil bastard. The time of reckoning was upon me, so I followed the flashes of light that were to lead me like shoots lead pigs to slaughter. Finally, I sat upon my mule at the end of the trial and faced T.P. in all of his evilness. He was dressed in all white with a matching white mask and he had a shoulder holster that housed a large caliber automatic with a silencer attached. In each hand was a twelve inch sterling silver dagger. I dismounted my mule and turned my back to T.P. as I began to tie the reigns to an adjacent bush. While my back was turned to T.P. chills ran up and down my spine. Even though I didn't believe he was ready to kill me so quickly, the thought| of being wrong terrified me. My senses were keen with anticipation of the unexpected. While my back was still turned, I heard the sound of something soaring through the air at a speed so fast that it whistled. My mind quickly told me that it was one or both of those silver daggers headed for my back. I quickly drove to the ground beneath my mule for cover. Seconds later before I could turn my head to see, my mule dropped top the ground upon my body. I quickly crawled from beneath the mule and turned to face T.P. who was holding only one silver dagger. My mule was killed instantly, so I knew that the other twelve inch dagger was embedded somewhere in the mule's head, but I dared not look. The sight might destroy what little nerve that I had left. I started walking towards T.P.

and I never looked back at the mule. As I approached T.P. he stared at me with penetrating effects that made me feel as if my soul was being x-rayed. The closer I got to him the more my body weakened. I was a frightened and borderline terrified, but worst of all, T.P. knew it too. He stood tall and straight and showed no signs of having and type feelings at all, even though his atmosphere was totally evil. As I stood face to face with T.P., I asked him may I see my daughters. About two minutes passed, before he replied. He instructed me to sit on the ground and pay close attention to what he had to say. He told me my daughters were safe for the moment but whether they lived or died would depend on how I performed.

"T.P. knelled down on the ground only inches away from where I sat and slowly raised his dagger upward until the point of the dagger was touching the center of my throat. I was frightened. No, No I wasn't frightened, I was completely terrified. I dared not stay still and I dared not move. The wind suddenly began to blow forcefully, and produce an evil howling sound. I knew then that I was no match for T.P. My mind couldn't think of anything that I could do, that my terrified body had courage enough to try. I was petrified and helpless. The wind began to lessen and loud howling sounds became very low pitched and sounded distant. The presence of evil was much too strong and I knew it could be felt miles into the bush.

It was at that time when T.P. looked me straight in my eyes while still holding the dagger to my throat. His hand never made the slightest movement, while in the center of his piercing eye I could see tombstones. Instantly after the silence and intimidating stare, T.P. asked me "Which of my two daughters do I love the most. He said if only I could have one of the two, which one would it be?

Henry's face began to turn flush and his breathing became deeper as his posture drooped over a nearby high back sitting chair. With eyes about to overflow and tears of pain Henry said "I love both of my daughters with all my heart and soul, I could never choose only one of them.

Only moments after Henry spoke the words that defined his equal love for his two daughters, Henry broke out in a painful cry that was full of tears, a runny nose and sounds of incurable agony. His friends quickly ran to his side to aide and comfort him. Henry was reliving his story as he told it, but in the process each word that he spoke was draining life from his soul and he was dying from verbal mental thoughts, that hit his heart like bullets being fired from a gun.

Jeff Wielder blurted out in a rage of pain and compassion, "Henry don't finish your story! You don't have to and we don't want you to. All of our pain and hurt stems from the lost of just one love one, but Henry you have lost three times as much. Your hurt is too much to bare for only one man, and we don't want to lose you.

Henry began to whimper out words that had the broken language of a toddler just learning to talk. "I die, I'm nothing whimpered Henry."

NO! No!, No!, said Lester as he continued to speak You are still the man that you always were. The things that you have endured would have totally destroyed the average man. Please don't give up and feel lesser than you really are. We are family now and this night is for us. T.P. will be destroyed for all times. We have Never stop believing in made an evil wrong right. yourself Henry for we are very proud of you. This toast of respect and admiration, I make for you. Henry, the man of men, Lester toasted with his glass held high.

Everyone joined in and moved closer to Henry to lay hands of affection upon him as they voiced manly gestures in his honor.

"What has taken place this night was achieved by all of us pulling together and acting as one. We shall stay as one and none of us will fall or weaken without immediate strength and aide from the next, " Jeff %3D spoke with his left hand holding his drink and his right hand extended. "Place your right hand on mine my friends one for all and all for one," Jeff concluded.

The words that had been spoken and the touches of admiration upon Henry's living corpse of a body began to take root and give birth to a gleam smile of self esteem upon Henry's hurt and pain carved face.

Thank you all so much my friends, No! Thank you my brother, that's what each of you are to me, Henry blurted out as he stared each of his newly made family eye to eye.

The room began to sing with the words "Brother! Brother! Family! Family! From the mouths of all the destroyed men of the newly made family.

I can go on now with my story of sadness, Henry said as he began to separate himself.

T.P. slowly removed the sterling silver dagger from my throat and began to rise to his feet. He stood tall with the look of being invincible, uttered Henry.

He told me that I can and will choose life or death for my daughters. T.P. explained that if I choose one, there is a possible chance that I can save one. But if I don't choose either one then both of my daughters will die right before my eyes. He then reached down grabbing a fistful of hair and snatched me to my feet while pointing to a path that lead to a clearing. I began to walk down the path in front of him and the evilness of his atmosphere made my body breathe a if I had been running miles. After about three or four minutes of walking, T.P. shouted, "Stop where you stand!" I did exactly as I was told and turned to face him. He walked slowly towards me until he was about four or five feet ahead of me. With an icy stare and evilish smile on his face, T.P. began to speak. He told me fifteen feet around the bend that I will have forty-five seconds to choose life for one of my daughters or death for the two of them. I could not imagine anything as horrible and painful as the choice that bastard was forcing me to make.

Do not move an inch from where you stand until I tell you to come forward, he commanded.

T.P. turned his back toward me and proceeded around the bend until he was out of sight. After he was out of sight, there was a lifeless silence that lasted for three or four minutes. The silence was draining the soul from my body. I felt so empty and lifeless. It was very hot and humid. My clothes were wet with sweat yet my body began to tremble with a teeth chattering chill. It was at this time when I hear him begin to speak to my daughters.

Baby girls, your father is here to save the day, but at most, he can only maybe save one of you. Who will it be? Who is daddy's pet? Your father says that he loves the two of you equally and he can't pick. I say bullshit! One of you means more and one you mean less. There are no two things on this earth that are equal or identical. It can be the same kind of shit, but it can never be the same shit. Your father has a choice to make, and there is no time allowed for him to fuck around. If he fucks around and don't go straight to his choice because being right means both of you are the same, then both of you bitches will die and he will hurt three times as much. Two hurts for the true one that he loved most and could have saved and didn't. Then the third for the lesser of his true love and his fake ass devotion to meaningless conformity.

Ever loving father you may come forward now, T.P. uttered in a cheerful voice. My heart began to beat rapidly as sweat dripped from my body like rain, Henry said soft and weakly.

As I began to come forward and around the bend, no words could describe the feeling bestowed upon me from the vicious horrible sight that I saw. Henry uttered slowly.

With sweat pouring from Henry's body, tears dripping from two reddish eyes and saliva filling his mouth, Henry tried to describe as best he could what he saw at the end of the bend.

I saw my daughters about forty yards apart, facing each other. They were in garbage cans that were chained to a tree.

The trash cans were galvanized and the lids were bolted to the can. He had cut holes in the top just big enough for their heads to stick through and I stood at the end of the bend an equal distance between my two loving daughters. They were crying and screaming with faces filled with terror. Father! Father!, Save us please. Don't let us die this death, please father.

Their words are still making crystal clear sounds throughout my mind, Henry said with a low key hoarse voice.

Each garbage can that held my daughters captive were half filled with gas and half filled with fumes. There was a trench that had been dug which connected the two garbage cans. It was about forty yards in length and about four inches deep. It too was filled with gas. I stood helplessly at the middle of the trench, about twenty yards from either of my daughters, uttered Henry as he placed his left hand over his mouth while lowering his head.

Henry began to pause and minutes of silence filled the room. No one could speak. Everyone was caught up in the mental painted picture of this awful scene. All heads began to shake from side to side as their faces began to droop. At least five minutes had past before another word was spoken.

It was at this time when Henry somewhat cryingly said; please stay with me my brothers. What I am about to say seems to take away my will to live. But, hard as it may be to finish my story, I will do so even if it kills me.

Henry began to recompose himself to that of an erect posture and slowly moved towards the center of his audience. The eyes of Henry's newly bonded family were filled with unexpected anticipation as they watched his every move. Henry's friends knew that he had suffered more and he had suffered harder than all of them. They had to bare the after effects of T.P.'s vicious terror, but Henry, he was made to watch and participate in a real life scenario created by one of hell's disciples. The room was filled with rage, hurt and despair with death haunting memories, but yet, there existed for this time only, a quiet still.

As I was saying before, Henry began to speak. I was standing at the center of the trench with two daughters facing each other about forty yards apart. I was basically twenty yards from either and both of my daughters were screaming my name for help. My two daughters that I raised from birth to adulthood. Both crying and screaming for me to be there for them and make the evil go away. Do you hear what I am saying? Can you really, really understand what that feels like?

Don't answer my friends. Just stay with me. I know that each of you do understand for we share the same vicious never ending pain.

It was at that moment when I lost and totally engrossed by what I was seeing and hearing that, that bastard T.P. spoke.

"Motherfucker, it's time to choose one your shit daughters to live or neither of them to live," T.P. spoke viciously as he pressed towards me as if he was a predator and I was his helpless prey.

With his left hand he stuck his sterling silver dagger to my throat. He had a half wet saturated cigarette protruding from his mouth. Even through my terror and dismay, I could smell gas like fumes coming from the cigarette. T.P. began to push upward with his left hand until the dagger pierce my throat. Small drops of blood began to ooze down my neck. I dared not even flinch.

With his right hand he gave me a cigarette lighter and said motherfucker light my cigarette and you better not burn me. I carefully lit the cigarette and it instantly bursted into flames.

Like hands of lightening, T.P. snatched the cigarette from his mouth and launched a round house kick that swept my feet from under my body and sent me flipping in the air until I landed face down on the ground. While still holding the firey cigarette, T.P. said you have forty five seconds to get up off your ass and choose. Almost momentarily after he spoke those vicious words, he dropped the firey cigarette into the gas filled trench. The unification of the fire and gas gave birth to seven or eight feet flames that towered high above me as if it were an unearthly human. The flame did not surge from side to side as I stared it down and tried to scramble to my feet. Instead it blew sand and dirt in my face and eyes. I quickly rubbed and shielded my eyes to maintain vision while erecting my body to full posture. Through my burning sand filled eyes, I could see the fiery flame thrust toward me as it smacked my body back to the ground with a blistering heat.

Believe me my friends, my brothers, when I say, with all my strength and will power, I could only raise my head. As I raised my head, that evil ass towering flame lowered itself to my eye level and seem to dance in a swirling motion directly in front of my face. I was totally helpless and there wasn't a damn thing I could do. It was at this time when I heard a powerful wind that seem to come out of no where. It sounded like it was a great distance away, but with each passing second, its faint howl became louder and louder, as it hurdled bushes in the air and rock trees from side to side. The cloud formation began to change until it hid the sun from view. The sky had darkened and the brightest light that could be seen for miles was the flame that danced in the gas filled trench before my weeping eyes. Almost instantly, that distant evil wind was upon me, as it screamed a howl that only could be made in hell. I saw the wind split the dancing flame half into. Like a bolt of lightening, the flame raced in both directions through the gas filled trench. Both of my daughters calling, screaming my name and begging for my help. I sprang to my feet and all I could see was two faces of terror screaming," Daddy save me! Daddy! Daddy! Help me please Daddy! Oh God what have I done, cried Henry as he dropped to his knees in pain and agony.

Jeff started toward Henry to aide and console him, but Henry threw up both hands in a pushing back motion, while yelling No! No!

Henry continued speaking by saying, I could not charge towards one of my daughters and put out that vicious flame without turning my back on my other beloved daughter. I cried out, Oh God NO! NO! As I fell to my knees with both palms of my hands covering my tear drenched face. Seconds later, I heard two back to back explosions that sucked the mind and soul out of my worthless body. I truly believed that I died that instant. Hours and hours had past before I gained consciousness. It was morning. The sun was barely coming up. As I opened my eyes and blurred vision began to focus. The first thing I saw was the face of terror tattooed my daughter's Stella face. She was about 10 feet away from me. Her head was separated from her body and her eyes were open as we stared each other eye to eye. In the background I could see the remains of Stella's and Belinda's body parts covered in blood and all twisted up in strains of meat and guts. Vultures and other scavenger animals were feasting and devouring my daughter's remains. Like a mad man, I began to chase them all away as I gathered my daughter's parts and placed them in one pile. I dug a shallow grave with my hands and the aide of a stick that I broke from the branch of a nearby tree. The head of my daughter Belinda, I never found.

After my grief and sorrow had deepened to the lowest level, my awareness began to come forth. It was then that I realized that evil bastard T.P. was nowhere in sight and no where to be found. I gathered myself as best I could to make the return trip back to the bush. As I approached my dead mule to get some supplies for the trip back, I observed a note pinned to my mule's neck with the second silver dagger. First I was hesitant to read it, for vengeance of his death was the only thing on my mind. I had no dignity, faith or love left in me. However, I snatched the note and read its evil contents.

The note read To the Bitch Ass Shit that couldn't choose. One of your daughters would have understood that you couldn't save her, but the other one that you could have saved and didn't should hate your punk ass forever. For now, live with it you bitch as motherfucker.

I thought that I couldn't be hurt any worst then I already was, but after reading that vicious note, .my heart began to pound and flutter. I began to feel very weak and faint, for those words were very harsh but most of all they were true.

What kind of man am I? I could have saved the life of one of my daughters and deep in my heart, I know they knew that. But instead, they watched me just stand there and fall apart while they screamed and begged me to save their lives. Oh God, what have I done? Please forgive me. My friends, I wish it was me dead instead of them. "You do believe me don't you," Henry cried out as he clutched the left side of his chest with both hands.

Henry's face became very flushed and his breathing deepen as he fell into the glass coffee table which was trimmed in 14kt gold. The table shattered into many sharp and jagged pieces. Before Henry's friends could come to his rescue, Henry was lying face down over the broken glass coffee table.

Henry's bonded friends began to hubber over him and carefully picked his fainted body from the broken glass table. As they laid him on the couch, Jeff Wielder shouted to his butler bring forth some drinking water and some cold wet towels.

As Henry's friends gazed down upon his limp body, they noticed that he was barely breathing and his face was very pale.

Jeff began to loosen Henry's shirt and tie as he shouted once more "Hurry up with the water and towels." The butler immediately bursted through Henry's friends whom circled around his fallen body. Jeff snatched the cold wet towels from his butler's hand and began wiping Henry's face and patting his forehead.

"Thomas trembled and fumbled to get his hands beneath Henry's head in hopes of raising him as quickly as possible. Just as Thomas had Henry's head and shoulders in his arms and proceeded to erect him to a drinking posture, Henry showed the face of a thousand agonizing deaths.

Henry clutched tightly the arm of Thomas with both hands and slowly, Henry opened his mouth to speak. Even though only a faint breath of air was expelled from Henry's mouth, his closely bonded friends could seemingly feel every word that Henry wanted to say as they watched Henry's eyes slowly roll back into his head.

Henry's friends began to shower their faces with a down pour of tears as they fell to their knees and placed their right hands across his freshly corpsed body. Not a word did any of the men speak and nor did they gaze into each other faces. They simply bowed their heads and each in their own silent way tired to absorb another painful newly opened non healing wound.

It was at this time in the midst of the quiet storm like silence, that the night wind blew a screaming, unearthly howl which forced the courtyard french doors to open and bang repeatedly against the wall until every window pane of its frame was shattered. Anicy chill filled the room as the men sprang to their feet while being totally engrossed with shock filled terror. The night wind began to lessen and its haunting howl began to fade. Suddenly, a low pitched explosion could be heard in the distance which caused Henry's friends to be even more startled as they flinched and nested closer together. As the remaining four men stared at each other, they could only see faces carved with terror. With a trembling voice and a shivering body Jeff Wielder said, "At last, it is done.

CHAPTER EIGHT

Jeff Wielder led his friends to the partially destroyed French doors and slowly began to stop. He gave distance of ten feet or more to the open doors as he and his friends viewed the damage from afar.

There was a full moon that brightly shined rays of light onto the broken window panes that laid scattered on the floor. Dark clouds began to drift across the moon lit sky and the darkness and the light began to clash. It gave birth to streaks of light and shadows that swirled and danced off the broken window panes throughout the room. Everyone in the room could feel a chilling Halloween like atmosphere a the night wind softly began to blow a howling melody of evil sounds through the broken window panes on the French doors.

Jeff and his friends began to exit the drafty room which was filled with illusions of terror and maybe fatal expectations of something yet to happen.

Jeff ordered his butler to secure and cover the broken French doors after which, he was to lock the entrance to the entire room. Even though everyone felt certain that T.P.'s eminent death was done and over; they still felt frighten and gravely unsafe.

As Henry's remaining four friends once more encircled his body, Lester removed his black tuxedo coat and placed it over Henry's face, shoulders and waist.

Jeff began to speak by saying, "Henry's death, sad and painful as it is to us, must bring us closer together and make us even stronger than before. We owe that much to our fallen brother.

To live through Henry's tragedy once, was more than enough to rob the average man of all of God's life giving necessities, said Lester as he continued to talk. In order for Henry to tell his heart breaking story, Henry had to retrieve it for a second time and to feel the awful hurt and devastating lost again was more than Henry could bare. Henry got caught up in the agony of it all and it proved to be fatal, sighed Lester as he dropped his head.

"AT least now our fallen brother can be a t peace," Thomas spoke softly.

Jeff began to conclude that after everything is over and we have cleaned up every trace of T.P's remains, then we will notify the proper authorities and have Henry's body picked up. Jeff caressed his champagne glass with the tips of his fingers and then held it high in the air. With a broken speech of a voice said, "We love Henry, may you rest in peace.

Everyone joined in and held there glasses high to give toast to Henry's homecoming to the after life.

Jeff began to approach his butler and affectionately placed his right hand on his butler's shoulder, while placing his drink of expensive champagne on the mantle with his trembling left hand. With an unsteady voice, Jeff Wielder told his butler to have the chauffeur bring the limo to the front entrance, for it is time to view the damage of the explosion and the remains of that bastard T.P.

He also instructed the other butler to summon forth Gibson who was the head of security. Jeff let it be firmly clear to his butler that he wanted to see them immediately and thus get on with the premeditated business at hand.

All of the remaining guest were just as eager as Jeff. They too wanted to see and know which of the horrible deaths did T.P. fall victim to.

As Jeff and his friends awaited the arrival of the chauffeur and the head of security it seem as if the men took one last final look into their past as they gave icy stares at the floor and walls. Dead silence filled the room as each man tried to bury their hurt and pain, once and for all.

Thomas broke the silence by saying, "I am beginning to feel better with each passing minute my friends. Soon all of this will be behind us and we can go forth with our lives."

"Yes", Lester said, once we close the door on this matter, we should never, never look backward at our part again.

Gibson interrupted Lester by his quickened entrance into the room. All heads turned toward Gibson as their sparkling eyes lighted his entrance.

After being unexpectedly pierced by an assortment of enchanted rageful hurting eyes, Gibson came to a dead halt and slowly began to focus on the unusual atmosphere contained in the room. He chose not to speak, but waited for further instructions to be given to him.

Gibson knew the part of this horrid drama that he was suppose to play. He knew that he had to act and respond to what ever lives ahead and with a man that is so evil as T.P., the thought of something going wrong was too terrifying. What if something or anything didn't go as planned. He knew that with T.P. no one gets a second chance.

Gibson silently prayed for inner strength and mentally convinced himself that there was nothing that could go wrong. After all, the plan was perfect. Gibson felt very positive about T.P.'s death and deep in his heart, knew it was the right thing to do. It was the only thing to do.

It was at that moment that Jeff broke Gibson's mental trance by saying, "Gibson, the moment of truth is at hand. I want you to send two cars of security to the scene and assess the damage and separate T.P.'s body from the debris."

I also want two cars of my security to accompany me and my friends in the limo. Gibson, I want you to be in my party and you will ride upfront in the limo beside my chauffeur.

"Gibson! Set the first two cars in motion and come straight back," Jeff said out of his mouth with tired of waiting restless eyes. Do it now Gibson, cause time is wasting.

Gibson began to turn and leave the room and Gibson knew by the tone of Jeff Wielder's voice, that the talk was over. The remaining guest began to move closer to Jeff and it was obvious that the feeling was mutual.

Jermaine said as he moved impatiently towards Jeff in the mixture of his other friends, "Let get it done once and for all. Fuck that got damn Bastard."

Damn right! Thomas said as he continued to talk. Let's end this shit now.

It was like an instant change of life, or maybe a second chance at life. Without warning and out of no where, the remaining four men stood bold and strong on their self declared mark. No doubt, the men had closed the door on the hurt and painful loss of the past.

Like a breath of fresh air that swept through their pain battered soulless bodies and leaving them all anew. It was unanimous with one and all, that they do it now and do it with a serious, vicious attitude.

As Gibson walked out of the newly changed hyper tense room, the chauffeur walked in.

"Sir Jeff," the chauffeur said as he stood face to face with Jeff Wielder. The limo is ready and waiting in the front entrance.

Wait in the limo Richard. I want to give Gibson a ten minute start. Keep the motor running and warm up the limo. My friends and I will be coming out to the car in about ten minutes.

It seem obvious that all things that were lost and discreditably taken away from the men had come back to them ten fold.

If there were any people ever more deserving of a blessing or just simple good great things to happen to them. Than there were none more deserving than Jeff and the remaining four knights in shining armor.

It was at this time in the night blanket of darkness, the self made brotherly group saw a pair of headlights leaving the guard gate entrance of the mansion slowly coming towards them.

All conversation began to cease as Jeff and his friends stared unto the approaching headlights. Everyone in the limo figured out and sorted that it could only be Gibson returning back to join and protect their party of five.

But still even though that was the most likely scenario, positive feelings began to give way to the negative feelings.

Jermaine, whom had nothing to much to say before, finally came out of his conclusions and began to speak.

"I'm really ready to move on this. I've finally emptied my gut my friends, my brothers and most of all my family. Let us all once and for all finish the game and get on with life.

Jeff Wielder said with a simple yes and continued to speak after a brief pause. Lets go and do what has to be done. Follow me my brothers to the limo and to the end of the road, the end of the line and finish it all.

Jeff began to lead his friends to the front entrance of the mansion where the limo with the motor still running sat parked waiting to be driven to the end of the line.

Jeff and his friends exited the mansion and took seats in the limo. Jeff ordered his butler to bring forth another unopened bottle of the expensive champagne.

While Jeff and his friends sat impatiently in the limo awaiting the expensive bottle of champagne and the return of

Gibson, they filled the car with manly chit chat and a robust feeling of a rewarding job well done.

Jeff and his friends had bleed and crawled their way back to the peak of their manhood. They sat in the limo and at the same time waiting with chilling anticipation to see if they were really right or fatally wrong.

The headlights began to come closer and closer to the limo as Jeff and his friends stared down the headlights until the lights stopped about fifteen feet in front of the limo.

The car stopped with the rear door of the vehicle slowly opening. As all eyes in the limo focused on every detail of the stopped car, it was if they had no pre knowledge of the car or its occupants.

From the opening of the rear door, a tall stranger began to emerge and deep down inside, everyone felt that it did not have to be Gibson in the car with the forth coming headlights. Just maybe everything had gone wrong and behind those headlights it was T.P. If that be the case, they would self destruct on their own. The terror of T.P. and what they tried to do with him and to him was more than enough to bare. To add failure on their part, or just the thought of failure would break each man down into a spineless, worthless pool of shit.

The car continued to come forth until it had stopped adjacent to the limo. The rear door on the sedan sprang open and Gibson began to exit the car.

Jeff and his friends gave a sign of relief as they leaned back into the seats of the limo to a more comfortable relaxing position. Gibson entered the limo and announced that the first team of security has already left for its destination. As a matter of fact said, Gibson, "They should be there by now and separating T.P.'s body from the debris.

Gibson continued talking and explaining to Jeff Wielder that they would pick up the second team of security that awaited them at the main gate to the mansion.

Jeff only nodded his head and picked up the car phone. Jeff began dialing numbers that connected him to his first team that was already at the scene. Immediately upon receipt of his phone call, Jeff asked eagerly, "Have you located T.P.'s body yet?

Jeff then gave an order to his security to keep him posted and they should be there in a matter of minutes.

Jeff told Gibson to take his place in front with the chauffeur and let's go to the scene straight away.

As Gibson exited the rear of the limo and reentered the front of the car, Jeff began to explain to his friends what had transpired on the phone.

As the limo pulled off it was joined by two other security cars as it exited the main gate.

Jeff told his eagerly awaiting friends that his security was extinguishing the fire in the Rolls Royce. He assured his friends that T.P.'s body was in the burning car because there are no signs of him making it out of the vehicle.

As the limo and the two security cars slowly drove down the lonely dark country road, the night wind began to play a tune full of horrid evil sounds as it blew through the over lapping trees that covered the road. The explosion seem to have triggered and destroyed the creatures of the forest that constantly move throughout the surrounding forest.

Although no animals could be seen, the rustling of bushes and the breaking, crackling sounds of twigs could be heard and noticed on both sides of the road. It seem obvious that at any time some large or small animals should jet across the road bound for the forest on the other side. But yet, not a creature was seen.

As the limo and the two security cars pulled up behind the two security cars that had come before them, Jeff and his friends rolled forward in their seats to get the best view possible.

The second team of security immediately exited the cars with weapons drawn formed a protected circle around the limo.

Jeff and his friends then exited the limo and were joined by Gibson as they slowly walked towards the shattered burned Rolls Royce.

As the men came closer to the Rolls they saw metal debris from the car and scattered small trees and bushes that were half burned with still a dying flicking flame.

Also partially burned was one of Jeff's killer Rottweiler. They could see his mouth completely wide open which showed his two inch dagger like teeth. The dog's head was lying in a pool of blood. It was very easy to see that the pool of blood didn't come from the explosion. Instead, the pool of blood came from the bullet hole between the eyes of the K-9 that was still flowing blood from the head of the dead killer dog.

The adrenaline was soaring high. Not just in the bodies of Jeff and his friends, but in all of the men who stood at the scene secretly expecting anything to happen at any given moment.

While still encircled by the armed body guards, Jeff and his friends slowly moved to the blown out windows of the Rolls Royce to see the remains that lied within.

The first thing that they saw were burnt fragments of the second killer Rottweiler. He was scattered all over the front seat in bits and pieces.

Also in the front seat of the Rolls Royce was a badly burned tuxedo coat with one of its sleeves still tied to the passenger side door handle. The other sleeve of the coat was closed inside the door jam of the driver side door with just enough of the sleeve stuck outside of the car door to hold one hand.

Except for T.P.'s coat there were no traces of him to be found inside the car. Even though shock and terror filled the lungs and bodies of all the men that stood upon the ground on that unearthly night, they still could quickly reason things into proportion.

It was obvious that T.P. used the one bullet he had to blow a hole in the head of the K-9 that laid dead in a pool of blood. He then tied his coat sleeve to the passenger's door and opened it while holding the other sleeve of his coat with his hand. With perfect timing, he allowed the other K-9 to enter the car through the passenger side door while he exited out of the driver side door at the same exact time. By doing so, he freed himself from the car and trapped the last remaining K-9 inside the car. All that remained was for him to clear himself from the radius of the explosion.

Without warning, Thomas busted into a loud scream and fell against the ruin Rolls Royce. We have fucked up royally this time; our lives are not going to be worth a shit cried out Thomas.

The bastard has gotten away and he is out there now somewhere, screamed Jeff.

It was at this time when the night wind began to blow fierce March like wind with an evil unearthly howl.

Jeff ordered everyone to get back in the car immediately. He was terror stricken and could feel evil and death all around him.

The sky began to blacken as the night wind made the trees sway from side to side. There were two blasts of thunder back to back and sharp streaks of lightening that cut a sixty foot pine tree down and laid it dead center across the Rolls Royce. It was fright beyond all comparison that each and every man felt when Jeff ordered everyone to leave immediately and return to the mansion. It seem to give a temporary form of instant relief.

Everyone knew that they had to finished the game and the game was going to be played on.

Silently in the minds of each of the men they concealed thoughts of death. In order for them to live T.P. must die. They all knew that death was eminent but they did not know for whom nor did they know when it would occur.

As the limo and the four security cars began to turn around and head for the mansion. Jeff and his friends looked through their windows with watery eyes and tears stained, terrified faces.

As the night wind rocked trees from side to side and howled, its evil sound was completely in harmony with the thunder in the blacken sky. One and all could see a pair of evil illuminated bedroom eyes disappear into darkness.

As heartbreaking and painful as all of this may seem or maybe it all means nothing unless someone can finish the game once and forever.

As Jeff's cascade of cars transported him and his friends back towards the mansion, the night wind lessoned it fierce winds and softened its evil howl as they all traveled down the lonely heartbreaking game not finished